M000188189

ALEX MORRALL

Adrift

The Storyteller and the Mosaicist

Copyright © 2022 by Alex Morrall

All rights reserved. No part of this publication may be reproduced, stored or transmitted in any form or by any means, electronic, mechanical, photocopying, recording, scanning, or otherwise without written permission from the publisher. It is illegal to copy this book, post it to a website, or distribute it by any other means without permission.

This novel is entirely a work of fiction. The names, characters and incidents portrayed in it are the work of the author's imagination. Any resemblance to actual persons, living or dead, events or localities is entirely coincidental.

First edition

This book was professionally typeset on Reedsy.
Find out more at reedsy.com

Looking for a book to get lost in..?

Sign up to my reader's club on www.alexmorrall.com for reading samples and updates, including information on Helen & The Grandbees:

Twenty years ago, Helen is forced to give up her newborn baby, Lily. Now living alone in her small flat, there is a knock at the door and her bee, her Lily, is standing in front of her. Read more on www.alexmorrall.com

Contents

Prologue

On a good day in Robin's life, on an ideal day which is creatively profitable, the world buzzes with the fact that he is a maker and not a subordinate, it fizzes with tangibility, and the pavement glows where the air hits it…

Or one of those days when Robin doesn't find himself skint and stranded in town at three o'clock the following morning.

On one of those perfect days, I believe Robin got up at eight (although this is conjecture) when the sun shone through the thin seventies-style curtains, shining off the gloss of the Kubrick poster, bringing the paler curves of the faces out in relief. He fished about for the jeans tangled on the floor and stumbled out to the bathroom to stand in the shower. And because it was such a fine day, the water springing against him was just the right temperature to refresh him. His hair washed clean in an astringent smell and body soaped in minutes, he climbed out and glanced at the grubby mirror fixed to the wall over the sink. He ran a wet arm across its steamed surface and briefly contemplated shaving. But you shouldn't waste the time of perfect days.

He grabbed at the pile of clothes on the floor. The T-shirt, he had left his T-shirt in the bedroom. Wrapped in a blue towel, he walked watery footprints across the landing to find the green cloth nearly pushed under the bed. He pulled it on, followed by brief towelling and the rest of his clothes. They rubbed uncomfortably against him where he was still wet. Then he thundered down the stairs. Perhaps barefoot? He could be wearing his trainers at this point, but that would mean that they had been in his room, reeking. Perhaps that makes sense, Robin's room full of day and night male scents, bloke stuff.

Wouldn't know, never been there. Only knew about the film poster because I was with him when he bought it.

Were his housemates still in, breakfasting, when he got downstairs? Half-watching gaudy breakfast TV and laughing at snatched jokes, brushing their hair in a mirror in the hall before leaving the house? I don't know what his housemates do for jobs, so I just have to guess.

But Robin had orange juice for breakfast on the pale square dining table, the sunlight still insistent through the plant-filled window ledge, bouncing off sea-green tiles on the walls. The orange juice was from the 'freshly squeezed' bottles even though he couldn't afford it. And he drank instant coffee (Gemma would never have approved). It was black. The milk had turned sour. He ate hot-buttered toast that leapt deliciously browned from the toaster and he thought about the bacon wrapped in the fridge, out of date tomorrow. But an ideal day is not a lazy day.

He dropped his plate and glass into the fading bubbles of the lukewarm washing-up water and took his mug upstairs with him to brush his teeth and collect his stuff. You know the sort of things. The sort of things that belong to artists, visionaries.

A few minutes later, the door clicked into its latch as Robin launched himself onto the balcony and ran down the steps to the street. The magician was out into the city.

I

Part One

Chapter 1

Ethiopian Street Scene, Copyright https://alexmorrall.com

Noel invited the stranger, who turned up a week late on our post-grad course, to the pub, where he sat buried into the corner of a cheap foam sofa, gathering himself to the open fire as if he was suffering from a persistent freeze that followed only him.

His ice put us on edge. It was only mid-autumn. We were hardly the most sociable bunch in the first place, reading physical geography, finding stories within the rocks of the land, but we'd no interest in excluding him.

I pushed a pint in his direction; some of the lager dripped with the motion. Girl buys boy drink. But it didn't feel that way right then. I was just trying to force down his tightened limbs. "I'm Bernie. It's Robin, right?' The man looked cold and dazed. Two cautious eyes lit by the flames of the open fire looked up. Something scared that didn't know its strength.

"No one here trusts you for not drinking."

He took the drink awkwardly. "I suppose I don't blame them." He sipped from the glass.

"Where did you come from? Most of us at least know each other by sight: halls, subjects, committees, mutual friends..." I trailed off, waiting for his answer.

He wiped his hand across his face. "I took a year out. Been teaching in Africa." He hesitated as if seeing a need to explain more. "I struggle to stay in one place."

"That'll explain the hunched shivering look before the winter."

He laughed lightly and made a visible effort to rearrange his shoulders. I felt grateful for this effort and warmed to him. "Not to mention the coat."

But he didn't take it off. "I got back yesterday..." He hesitated as if suddenly deciding that I didn't want to hear all this, but I nodded him on, and he gave a small smile before continuing. "Thirteen hours of high altitude, elasticated socks and menus on a yellow card."

"Jet-lagged?"

"And..." he began, leaving the word lingering, as if unsure whether or not to follow it up. "They say, when you come back, that things might not be normal, straightaway." He pulled a palm across his face as if it would bring him into normality. "Just, all those sights. I close my eyes and I see faded posters for the Sheraton and Hilton at passport control and hear the hum of insects in the hot crisp darkness." He blinked slowly.

Again, I had to nod him into continuing.

"The crescent of the moon lies on its back out on the other side of the equator. That's what I see when I close my eyes, the moon upside down in a red sky over the eucalyptus-lined hills and mountains." He rolled his shoulders and looked at his phone as if to stop himself rambling. "I suppose that here never felt that normal either, to be honest."

The honesty startled me. I enjoy being on the outside, but I find people on the outside usually make efforts to pretend not to be, striking the casing of a world they don't understand and just alienating themselves even more. It's different for me. I might not be part of my environment – a story that I'm never part of – but I do understand it, sometimes explaining it to the people inside when they have got tangled up with its undulations, helping them to unpick their way back in.

"I hear you've got a good rep, though. Good at data." His sudden change in topic, an echo of a charm that might be more vital if he were less jet-lagged, also felt like he was trying to avoid the glare of attention.

"What a compliment."

He smiled. "I saw you in the lecture earlier. You can look at the information and find the story to make sense of it, to make it come alive."

More than flattered at 'having a rep', I was taken aback at how his summary resonated with me. That's who I am, the narrator of the outside world but never part of it. I like it here, being able to make sense of everything around me but not hurt by it. 27b's music suddenly merged from the imitation of the sound of underwater to a deeply insistent dancing jazz. There were whoops from the bar and a chairless area in one corner was filled with a collection of dancers. I saw Robin smiling and gestured towards the dance floor with my eyes. "Come and meet the others."

He glanced down at his huddled body. "I think it would be easier just to watch for now."

"Nope, that's not a thing. If that was a thing you could have just watched documentaries about Africa on the TV."

"I…"

"You can't just watch."

He smiled. He took off his coat. He took the glass and sipped from it as I watched. Then he placed the glass on the table and took my empty hand.

Another whoop. "Hey, Bernie's on the dance floor." I smiled at the darkness where it came from, unable to make out any face. The voice sounded like Mark's. Well, they should have introduced themselves to the stranger.

As Robin stood beside me, I realised that he was taller than I had at first thought. And some of the residue of his personality was still living in England because his body was fitting into the rhythm against me, pulling me into the music, to enjoy its magic.

Girl dances with Boy. I did sense it then, but I dismissed it.

We landed on seats at the four-person table, eight of us crowded about it. Now I had broken the ice, everyone wanted to know who the cold-looking man was. Sophie and Luke were already folded into each other, but graced Robin with a temporary parting from each other's lips to say words like, "It's Robin, isn't it? What do you think of the course so far?" and not listen to the answer. Gradually, the group uncrumpled who Robin was, glimpsed the mislaid spirit before we coiled off into debates about art and science.

At closing time, he pulled me back and whispered to me.

"Do you think I'm alright?" His eyes were reaching out for an answer with an impossible honesty. I could smell the beer on his breath.

"Alright?"

"Settling back into the UK again; finding my identity here."

"You'll get there. The witticisms will gradually overcome the inappropriate laborious answers to questions."

He looked a little serious, downcast at the criticism, but then his face cracked with laughter and I realised only when it was broken, the proximity we'd had to each other.

I didn't worry about it too much.

Chapter 2

A couple of weeks after meeting Robin my own 'other world' started to interrupt my new home – news of a brand-new baby brother and requests for me to go home to see him. No matter how much I tried to detach, make it a story from my past, home would keep dragging me back and so I found myself sleepless on a flying visit to see my dad and his wife, Eleanor, who I hadn't got around to seeing in nearly a year – and my little brother who I had never seen before.

My journey took three hours. The falling in and out of sleep between stations made it seem even longer. By the time I reached home, I was hypnotised by travel. I didn't want to stand up as the rooftops of my village came into view.

In the past, I would have made this journey dutifully many times in the year. Then, after the marriage, my excuses had been more easily accepted. They, Dad and Eleanor, expected that I would come home in the end, anyway. After eighteen years growing up in the house with just me and my dad, they must have assumed that I was dependent on their world.

The station near home had just two platforms, two directions. The floor outside the ticket office was cold and tiled red and the double doors to the station were yellow. The whole area was glowing with autumn sunlight.

I had never been met at this station. It was a short walk from the station to the house on the corner of the road and all my feelings rose as I walked it, as I turned the bend in the road to see the house slide into view, as I walked the garden path, as I scraped around in the seed box in the porch to find the door key, getting dry soil in my fingernails. The scent of home. I leaned on the door to push it open as I heard the key click. In the hallway, I called hello, and tugged my bag in through the front door.

There was no immediate reply, so I moved into the front room. Eleanor was there, sitting on the chaise-longue, a newspaper supplement in front of her. Her long mousy hair trailed down her back, looking unbrushed but gleaming all the better for it. The odd silver strand had developed since the pregnancy. Eleanor was beautiful, tall and unusually slim. That day, she looked ghostly, exhausted but happy. Eleanor was thirty-four, first kid.

She looked up as I hovered at the door. The room was lit by both a small window onto the road, and a small lamp in the corner, under which Eleanor had been reading. Both colours of light reflected in small points on Eleanor's eyes. Every corner of the room escaped light. I said hi, again. There was a need for some kind of politeness here. One of us was the guest. She looked as if she was going to invite me in to sit down but then thought better of it. I took the lead, walking to the armchair and slouching into it. "Hello, Bernadette," she said with traces of a Canadian lilt still left after a decade of the UK. It was a sign of nerves, calling me Bernadette after all the time that she had been there. She knew I was as Bernie as *Topcat*'s sidekick. She normally got over it when I'd been around for a while. "How's your masters coming along?"

And Dad called "Hi!" before I could answer her. The voice came from the block of light, beyond the hallway, that was our oversized scruffy kitchen. I could see a little of its light through the dining room beyond the red-bricked arch. I returned the greeting and he then continued to make cooking noises in the kitchen, humming *A Hard Day's Night*. He would be glad I was back – in spite of everything.

I turned to Eleanor, untying my trainers and discreetly putting them to one side next to the armchair, trying to make my presence in her life as invisible as possible. "Masters, yes. You know, last term stress, etc." The trainers looked scruffy in the room. Dad had never had a problem with me doing that, but I was suddenly conscious that it wasn't the same anymore.

Eleanor wasn't looking at the shoes. She smiled distantly. "That's nice." She seemed to be staring at the paper in front of her, but I think that she was dozing because the corner of the page was bending over and she didn't seem to notice. She would normally have made such an effort. I had never seen them this way before, so steadily lethargic. I was glad that they didn't seem to have the enthusiasm left to devote to my return.

She'd changed her life to be here. Once, she was choosing jobs, choosing houses, and boyfriends and parties and then suddenly she became my dad's wife.

Going through the process of return, the journey, the awkwardness of saying hello again, was a succession of images of another world, like a dream with a chronology that ploughed on regardless of whether I left or slept. Like sleep, this world occasionally succeeded in grabbing me back and then releasing me with dreamlike memories which shuddered into life during the late strained hours.

I grabbed at a glossy supplement just as Dad came in from the kitchen, holding a flask. He wore tracksuit bottoms with a T-shirt and an apron. "Bernie. Hello!" he cheered, again. I sat in the armchair, my knees brought up to my chin. I beamed up at him, moving my feet back to the floor. He turned to glance at Eleanor who was getting up from her seat. "Did you have a good journey?" He smiled. The corners of his eyes wrinkled in a way that was so Dad.

I affirmed that I did. Told him that I even did a bit of studying on the train.

"Good." He was sounding genuinely pleased, then he looked at the flask in his hand. "Anyway, you can have your cup of tea – white no sugar – in the car. You're in perfect time, but we want to get back to him as soon as possible." He kissed me on the cheek. "It's good to see you again."

There was a gleaming new people carrier in the driveway. All that for just one tiny baby. Dad jumped into the front, opening all the doors. After a pause, I climbed into the back. Central locking was something of a novelty to me after my friends' student cars. We waited for a couple of seconds in the plush décor of the car. I fished for the flask on the front seat. A warm drink, after all that travelling, seemed quite welcoming, even if I had to drink it out of a plastic cup. I sipped at the steam. Eleanor still hadn't left the house. Dad jumped back out of the car, into the house, "Just to check that's she's okay," leaving me to admire how the car sound system was superior to my tinny speaker at home. Two minutes later, he re-emerged, arm around her. Did he help her into her seat, help her with the seatbelt? I don't remember, but it would not have seemed odd. I was slightly happy because of his care, the understanding he exuded into her silences. He loved her.

I didn't get to hear the posh CD player's fine-tuned acoustics. We were a family. We were meant to be talking so Dad didn't even try putting it on. We weren't wordless in the car, but our words were idealess, exchanging pleasantries. Too many emotions fuzzing in the air to try and form into words.

Then there was the white hospital – bright lights – why was it that the whole world seemed to be offering this sharp light everywhere? Tall hospital doors.

Then coloured rooms – nursery rooms, 'A Picture for Mummy' papered rooms – little red chairs.

Then pale rooms again. Glass windows onto glass boxes, one of them containing Freddie. (Bernie and Freddie. Dad, did you do this name thing on purpose?) Little, more tiny than anything, more tiny than he should be. Hopelessly harmless and dependent – and compared to my natural insomnia, interestingly asleep.

I felt something. Wondered if it was love. Knew I had to keep

13

away from this place.

"They don't know how soon we will be able to take him home, Bernie." Out of the passing, memorised images of this early time, those are the only words I can remember from the hospital.

At home, conversation, food. A meal at home – not fast food, or dinner party, or cheap improvisations. More conversation. Money, exams, we're proud of you, do you remember so and so? Looking forward to you coming home this summer.

But it was too late by then. I knew I loved Freddie. It was the final decider, simple, a reality slithering towards me, and pinning my eyes with its own.

Sometime, Dad, I've got to tell you.

I declined help in tugging my bag up the stairs. I was the fittest person there. I left the open suitcase on my bed, bringing my life back into the old room, and started working my way down the winding stairs for coffee. I kept my feet on the wide side of each step, where there was still bare dark wood and my foot was smaller than the step. Me and my clumsiness, it took ankle acrobatics. What if I misstepped? What if Dad, or Eleanor misstepped? How many times did the thought have to cross my mind? I reached the bottom, the wider steps. Dad was clinking plates, piling them into the kitchen. There was the mumble of passing conversation between the kitchen and the dining room. I wondered how other people could live like this, how cosy, how terrifying.

What if someone were to die?

I slept out of politeness. Sleep seemed to come very easily upon me for once. Funny, considering the nightmares I was having in the early evening. That night, there was sleep and a six o'clock train in the morning, because I had to be back for, er, something. Well, it was nearly my finals, so I couldn't miss lectures.

They were asleep when I got up. I knew they would be. Why did Dad have to insist that I woke him to say goodbye? I knocked on the door, reticently. I was already in my coat, my bag on my shoulder. Dad came to the door after the period of time it would take to put on slippers and a dressing gown. He must have woken instantly. "It's all right," he whispered slowly closing the door behind him. "I was awake. Early morning sunshine."

"You weren't," I hissed.

He smiled.

"It was good that you came to see Freddie."

I shrugged, embarrassed,

"Did you like him?" he asked stupidly.

It wasn't the time to tell him about the love and its implications. "Sure."

He smiled at me. "I would give you a lift to the station, but I really don't want to wake Eleanor."

"No. Don't be silly," I interrupted him. "I don't need the starship to take me anywhere. I already have style."

He ruffled my hair. "Have a good journey." He kissed me goodbye.

Chapter 3

You know what magicians do?

They throw light across the skies in good times; they are friends with kings and queens; they temporarily lose their powers, maybe trapped by stronger forces in distant lands. They are significant to the stories, but they are side characters. The real stories are made up of battles or courtships or comings of age. So, Robin and I, the narrator, could both share our otherworldliness on campus while everyone else did the things that made the world turn around. We could still be the outsiders.

Still, it was hard to always remember with Robin that I was here to only tell other stories. I wondered if my love could ever be good enough for a story.

Our friendship progressed slowly from that first meeting in the obscure bar. I hardly saw him again for a few weeks. He'd look like he thought he'd have to explain himself to me if I bumped into him on the street. "I meant to come to that tutorial, but I was working on something." He'd look vaguely into the distance as if the horizon held the secret to stepping back into himself in Africa. When I laughed, it was like it brought his feet into the ground and he remembered where he was.

"What are you working on?"

He looked embarrassed, his cheekbones reddening again. "Project," he muttered, trying to back away from what he had just opened up. "Nothing really. I shouldn't have mentioned it." But somehow, from the rambled notes and diagrams that he did bring to tutorials, I knew it would be magic. "Can I borrow your notes from last week?"

Gradually as the weeks passed by, he would start to look like he could see out of his eyes without windscreen wipers and make lectures within the first opening moments. He'd start to tell me a bit about his trip abroad in the way he'd started to in the pub: Mercato's tents, sheltering pools of ground spices, yellows and reds clean on the dusty floor; the bustling straw baskets in traditional red and white, priced at ten birra, falling to one birra for three in the blink of an eye; and the following of children intrigued by his white skin, calling "Hello, Americanne," from tringing bicycles.

We'd find ourselves lingering longer and longer in the lecture room until eventually he said, "I think better when I walk. Can we just take a walk and let our brains work right?"

It seemed natural to walk down to the tourist centre of Warwick together. It was out of season. We saw the souvenir shops and walked along popular village roads. It was true that he thought better when we walked; he was more at ease with himself. "I need ways of processing things," he told me. "Walking and..." but he didn't finish the sentence.

The following week we did the same again, sometimes throwing in a long lunch. "You're not messing up as bad as you think you are," I tried to tell him. I'd noticed how he looked at the land, how occasionally he would pick up a rock or a stone and hold it as if he was learning its life in its cracks and eroded curves, as if his skill was to let the stones whisper to him, as evocative as his stories from Africa which he seemed to be struggling to leave behind. Sometimes, as we left some field trip, I would look back at the specimens he had left behind, but they were not just deserted, they were somehow arranged into loose sculptures of their own, telling abstract stories of emotions, maybe Robin's own distance.

"I don't think on my feet," he laughed at his own contradiction. "Well, I think on my own walking feet, I just don't think at speed when being quizzed on the spot."

Each time we drank glasses of wine before pulling apart at the railway at the last possible moment.

It was only after that time going back home that the conversation changed. We'd seldom talked about life outside of university. I'd been comfortable with that. No one wanted our stories. But the journey home had changed my tempo. He could see it in my gait, and I knew he was going to ask. "You know how, at university, we don't always talk about where we

18

come from…" Robin started eventually. "What happened? At home, I mean? You never talk of home."

I shrugged. "Well, there's a daddy and a step-mum, and a baby half-brother who's just been born a little early." I gazed into a shop window full of cakes with delicately crafted icing. The day was so bright, I could hardly see through the glare on the window. I could see Robin's reflection.

"Better than half a baby brother…"

I didn't mind Robin's probing. I didn't get the feeling that he was about to cross the line. He kind of nodded into the cake shop, as if to say, why don't we try it. We stepped inside and found it completely empty. Small cards of sticky laminated menus sat between salt and pepper pots.

"What about your mum?" He picked up one of the menus, still standing, and passed one to me.

"Died in a car crash with big sister when I was two."

"Sorry." He paused. "You're worried then?" he asked.

"About Freddie? I suppose. People could get hurt."

"People?" he asked, with a slight snort.

First Eleanor and Dad, then Dad more because of Eleanor and then Eleanor because of Dad and it all just carries on. "Yeah, dangerous things, babies. But it might all be fine. How about your family?"

"Okay." He tried to shrug but moved awkwardly underneath his collared navy T-shirt. I wondered if this was a natural response to my questioning of a subject we had never gone near. Maybe he needed the separation in his life too. "Do you get on with your stepmother alright?"

I nodded.

"Funny," he said, but he didn't explain and I winced.

"Sorry, was that rude?" He looked guilty and put his menu

19

down. "I wasn't trying to pry."

I didn't know how to explain, and said nothing, wondering if he had a stepmother with a different story, but I was too scared to ask. In fact, I realised then that my closed life was similar to his hidden project and half-finished explanations.

He scratched his forehead, frowning at the table. He didn't apologise again. I could see his face crowd with thoughts of what could be said. We weren't meant to talk about ourselves. I absently reached to the corner of the table to steady myself from the talk of family.

"I don't know her that well. I never will. I shan't get the opportunity."

He didn't push it, as if something more pressing had just crossed his mind.

Beyond the till, the missing member of staff blustered in. "Can I help with the menu at all?"

I was just about to lift my head and answer when I felt Robin's hand brush my fingers. I lifted my hand, thinking he could not have realised I was there, but his didn't move. He tutted softly, disappointed at the sound of the waitress' voice.

Does electricity pass both ways? Could Robin feel my belief in his magic come through in that touch? He was still slipping the backs of his fingers against mine and now I knew it was deliberate, and when I looked up, he was looking directly at me, in the middle of the café, watched by the waitress and the clanging dishes, ignoring them.

And my phone rang.

I lifted the phone from my pocket to see home's number flashing on the screen. For some reason, talking to my dad in front of Robin felt like an uncomfortable mix of two worlds. "I'd better take this." Robin's hand fell away. I looked around me for somewhere to talk that would not be overheard. "I'll just pop out for a few moments."

I hit answer as I reached the door and was surprised to hear Eleanor's voice at the other end. I tried not to sound confused.

"It's your, your..." she sounded equally confused.

"Dad?" I asked.

"Yes." There was a pause. I wasn't going to jump to conclusions. Why was Eleanor able to talk to me on the phone and not Dad? I wasn't going to worry without reason. "He would have called you himself, but he's on the motorway." I felt relief.

"What's wrong?"

"It's your, your..." This time I really didn't know who she was getting at. Maybe Eleanor just frequently forgot people's names.

"It's your grandmother."

"Oh, I see." Then I saw more. "Is she okay?"

Silence. It wasn't fair of Dad to make Eleanor make this call. They were reeling me in again, already. But this time it was inappropriate to wonder if it was all planned to get me back.

I looked through the windows of the cafe and watched Robin move from the counter to pick up some cutlery. He didn't look up. What made him do what he did in the cafe just now? The cake-filled windows started to spot with drizzle, and I saw him move farther away from me, more obscured by the droplets. But we had begun with that distance, so why did it bother me?

Chapter 4

"She won't feel any more pain, Bernadette. Think of it like that." I had reached the hospital earlier than expected. Dad was still on his way. That's how I ended up in this conversation, cringing at the obviousness of the 'comfort' I was being offered. I couldn't work out where my irritation was coming from, bouncing off the floor tiles and NHS blue walls, the sounds of steps on the corridors and whispers of passers-by. Was it the interruption of that moment with Robin? Or arriving at the hospital too late to say my goodbyes, being offered these mundane sympathies?

"So do I –me and Dad – call people, or do you guys deal with all that?" Death, the proof of it, the rituals of it, how does one go about it?

The nurse looked taken aback. I wondered if I should point out that the death of a grandparent is usually a person's first experience of such things.

"I think that the family arranges the undertakers."

He 'thinks'. Half my head wanted to laugh that the nurse 'thinks'. The answer, I supposed, was no surprise. This was a hospital, after all, proof of death available from the machines like fast food. Don't know why I asked really.

It seemed that I was expected to say something else then because he still sat near on the bobbling chairs leaning towards me. I was holding the plastic tea in my hand that he had insisted I took before telling me. As if the words, "I need a quiet chat, take a seat, and here's a cup of tea," aren't a direct translation for, "She popped her clogs before you got here, sweetie. Sorry and all that." That's the way I'd needed it to be, informative, civil and distant, not inviting emotion.

But I had been complicit. I had taken the drink and the seat. Didn't have the heart to make his careful orchestrations redundant. After all, the poor guy did this for a living.

The nurse was still sitting there. I hate uncertain behaviour. What would they do in a hospital drama? I wanted to say, "Hey look at us," to break the silence, but he'd think I was hitting on him – we were the right age. And I wasn't, by the way, hitting on him that is. That medicated look. Not attractive.

I could have said, "I've only just come into town. I haven't even spoken to my dad, yet," and point to the hastily packed backpack that had fallen over by my seat. I could have said, "I'd only just got back after visiting my little brother. Two visits home within three weeks, the definition of excess," but it would all require some sort of trust in this professional.

Eventually, the nurse smiled sympathetically and squeezed my arm which I figured was my dismissal. I wondered if the hospital had got through to Dad and Eleanor to tell them the news. Phones were supposed to be switched off so if they'd called, I wouldn't have known. I would have to sit around the waiting room, people-watching, feeling daft.

I got up and headed for the toilet, eventually finding the sign indicating that they were only a yard or so from where I stood. While the waiting room had at least pretended to look nice, with a few bright paintings on the olive walls, the toilets didn't even try. Bare and cold.

I was sick in the toilet – must cut down on those vending machine cups of tea – so I was there for longer than I thought, in the cubicle next to the one with a huge pool of what I hoped was just water on the floor. I leaned my head on the gloss-painted metal wall in an attempt to steady myself, and then lifted it suddenly at the thought of how recently the toilet evidently hadn't been cleaned.

There was just a tiny white flake of soap on the sink and the water from the taps didn't seem to want to warm up, making the room degrees colder than it really was. The hand drier whirred and softly breezed at my fingers.

I escaped to the corridor outside, having to give way to a wheelchair, two lollipop-lipsticked children and a host of nurses, and saw Dad at the other end of the waiting room. He looked up straight away.

"Bernie, I'm so sorry. The hospital rang just as I left the house and I couldn't get you on your mobile."

He already knew. I didn't have to tell him. We didn't have to talk about it.

"I'm staying at Grandma's. Eleanor has stayed to look after Freddie. You've brought staying-over things? It's probably easier if you stay here for a while now."

Eleanor couldn't make the funeral because of Freddie. So, it was just me and Dad, gone up to stay in Grandma's huge riverside house for the weekend and a bit. Proximity and emotion, just piling on. No way out. I couldn't avoid my own grandmother's funeral. We were as close as you might be: Granny and Granddad and the little girl who was so much like the little girl they once lost. Didn't they tell me so, visit after visit? Granny was the last of the two. They had desperately spoiled their only surviving grandchild.

It had been a stroke, her second, not so many months after my grandfather's heart attack. Dad had arranged an early funeral. I had four days to plan to leave, two days to worry that I would hurt Dad by not listening to his head. Then I worried whether I would hurt him with what I had to tell him. I would have to tell him, this time. It would be unfair of me not to say it in all of that time we were about to spend together.

We sat watching a film on TV the night before the funeral. We had bangers and mash on our laps. The room was mostly dark. That's the countryside for you.

"Everything's happening so quickly for you, Bernie," he told a commercial break that I was actually quite getting into.

Too quickly for me? It wasn't my son, my wife, my mother. Not for me. I just tumbled along, largely untouched.

25

He sighed. I worried for a moment he was going to hit the mute button on the TV, but instead, the ad break finished, and he muttered, "We should take the raft out, you know."

We walked along the wooden pier at the bottom of the garden. The evening was so golden sunny, appropriate to the nostalgia of a house I spent school summer holidays in. Tied to a pole at the end of the pier was Dad's most prized possession – a raft he had made in his late teens, younger than I was now. He loosened it and we both climbed on. I had a tartan travel rug in my hands that I draped over it, as he pushed us away from the pier so that we were held by the water, safe by the tether. Years ago, before the accident, before I came along, he would have detached it entirely, left us adrift in what after all is only a calm stream but I guess when you lose people close to you, you acquire these cautious habits.

He laughed at me with the rug. "Splinters, huh? You're just like your mother."

Oh, Dad no. Not mothers as well as dead grandmothers and premature babies. It was too much. I said nothing, shifting onto my back to let the brightness of the sky between the trees penetrate my eyelids. I sensed him doing the same, at the other end of the raft, so we lay, crown to crown, father and daughter and I could be a kid again.

"Freddie doing okay?" I regretted that I had waited to ask him this when I couldn't see his face. I had avoided eye-to-eye contact when I wanted to talk about something serious. Then I wished I could have caught that transient look of love that would have flickered across his face, unknown to him. Just as I interpret data, I would have looked at it as a scientist looks at a specimen, something I could learn the mechanics of but never really understand.

"Yeah," he half-sighed. "I think that everything is going to be okay."

Silence again. The sun became more golden as the minutes flickered past. The raft lilted gently, all the soft sounds of the stream around me. Dad broke it. "Bernie?" I knew he wasn't asking a question. He was inviting one. This little trip was because he knew I had something to say.

"I can't stay." I had said it. My mouth was dry. I knew immediately from the sound of nothing that he knew what I was talking about. I was waiting, thinking for him to ask me why.

Ask me why.

But he said, "It just seems silly. It's such a large house. Your room has always been there. Eleanor doesn't have a problem with it. Freddie assured me over coffee the other day that he'd love you to be around." He trailed off. I tried to laugh, but it was too soft, sounded more like a sigh. "There's good transport links once you get into town, thousands of places for you to work for." He paused again, but I didn't respond. "What if you don't find a job straight after graduation. You haven't got one yet, have you?"

"It doesn't work like that." Ask me why.

"I mean I understand wanting to go and find bright lights, the big city, but you belong with us."

Don't tell me why. Ask me why.

"Bernie. I don't understand. Why do you have to go?"

It was too late. My bravery had all gone. I tried anyway. "Dad, I told you about the…" I searched for the words. "It's like burning. I have to go. I can't stay with you."

"We've been through this all before. I thought that you had

changed your mind, agreed to stay with us for a little while, at least."

"I know, I know. It has just got more acute lately. And now seems a good time. You can start your life with Freddie and Eleanor. I thought…" I didn't pursue the line and he didn't encourage me. I thought Eleanor had turned up after all those years because Dad had known I had gone after my university life. Dad had known that it was time to move on.

"My little girl's leaving for the city where the streets are paved with gold," he mused to the sky. Because I had told Dad that the burning was about seeing the world, running away to see the fairy-tale city.

I couldn't tell him what it was really about.

What it was 'really about' was simple enough. It came from that cold and icy day years ago when my mum and big sister left in the car for a journey that they never came home from. Not that I remember the day, I was far too young. By the time I was three, the only memories I was certain of were the photos. But I remembered that day's ripples affecting the world around me during the following years.

Gently, growing up, I absorbed those ripples, the neatness after the tragedy. The emptied room and crisp cleaned sheets of what would later become Freddie's room, good enough for guests. Family friends came to help out and scare away all the cobwebs that no one had worried about before. I watched my dad put on weight, then lose too much weight, as if this was just how a normal family was.

And my young mind cleared out all the sadness as it matured.

I learned from that. Someone had gone from my life. I didn't remember them. I didn't hurt but I saw other people hurt and here's the logic: if you don't become part of the story, if you don't get close, stay outside and watch the story unravel, you don't hurt.

In the dark, I flicked through the numbers on my phone knowing I was only looking for Robin, my magician. I tried to think of reasons to avoid applying the truth to my relationship with Robin, the truth that if I gently pushed the raft away no one would get hurt. I couldn't click on his number.

A person might just say that I was sealing myself out of Dad's new family, Eleanor and Freddie, because I was scared of losing people, or hurting people; that I was too afraid to let myself love Robin; that I made myself the storyteller because I'd learned that's the safest place to be. But things just aren't that neat.

I'd admit, the reason I had to leave was the insistent fear of wondering who'd die next, calculating whose death would cause the least hurt. But also, it was the confusion and energy of making myself into that new family, loving new people. All that unpractised emotional energy.

And I wasn't afraid to love Robin. I did love Robin. I loved loving Robin, holding onto that glassy altruism, believing I had finally hit an absolute. But you see, I was the storyteller. Complete as my love was, I didn't have a right to it. Surely, it would have scared him if he knew because he wouldn't see the reasons. He'd think I'd be lying to myself.

And I didn't make myself the storyteller, I just was.

The way I saw it was, I wasn't unhappy. I'd seen blacker days. Why go about making things for myself to lose?

Chapter 5

Robin's bike was missing from the bike racks, I noticed, as I walked to the library when I got back. I resisted checking up on him by text. The journey from his halls to here was so safe, I told myself, just the occasional passing lorry. But as the hours ticked by, I still did not see it from the library window. It was easier to think about whether he was safe or not, than decide what to do about the moment in the coffee shop. There was too much to keep afloat.

Eventually, he arrived in the evening, his bike capturing the oranges and reds of the evening sun. He did not see me, and he looked so peaceful, quietly rolling in, and that felt like the final defeat. I couldn't carry on like this; I needed to tell him sooner rather than later.

I packed up my books then and there, and made my way down the stairs, bracing myself for the moment I might have to explain.

The pavement leading down to the library's double doors was damp with an earlier drizzle, and the sunlight was damp with the near dusk. The doors opened, and it took a moment for him to see me.

When he did, he smiled, but I couldn't bring myself to return it. "Getting a coffee. Want to come?" he called to me, gesturing to the student building across the pathway, and I agreed.

The evening had cleared the coffee shop of any other students and the dark was just starting to clamour up the windows. "Good time back home?" he asked me as we waited for the espresso machine to charge out our coffees.

I smiled my false smile. "Yeah, I suppose."

He glanced at me, clearly deciding not to challenge the likelihood of this. Two little white china cups and saucers of coffee were breezed in front of us. I'd started to doubt if I should have joined him. I looked at the cup as I sipped, to fill the silence. I had left a pink smudge of gloss onto the white. I sipped some more. In the past, we'd grab a coffee together without a second thought, but the moment in the café in Warwick had made me more nervous, worried he could see this could be mistaken as a first date.

"Nice coffee," Robin murmured into his cup.

The taste of mine was bitter.

The fluorescent lights in the room started to brighten against the near night. "I'm not enjoying it." I dropped it to the saucer noisily. Brown liquid spilt onto the white. I shivered.

"What's wrong" He frowned at me, suddenly attentive.

"Just claustrophobic."

He nodded and put his cup down too. He seemed to know what I meant, seemed to feel it too. "Well, you know how I prefer walking," he said, and the decision seemed to enliven him. He stood up, straightening his tall, tall legs, swinging his coat about him. I watched him mounting to his feet and then stood up to walk outside.

There weren't many people around outside, no one to confuse us for a couple when we strode out. I could sense his head was clearing with the walk and I was getting the impression that he had something to tell me. "The thing is," he started, and I waited because it felt like this was a new story, a new discovery about Robin. "I can't stay here."

I was confused, but relieved we were not going to talk about the moment in the café in Warwick. But most of all, I felt the cold grow colder. My lack of contact, my lack of smile meant that we weren't even going to acknowledge the moment in the café. And worse, he was leaving.

"You're shocked?" he said to my non-response.

I shrugged. I found it harder to keep pace with him as it all sank in. "I suppose not." Now he'd broached it, I realised the signs had been around for weeks. "You were pretty distracted on that last field trip to the rocks at Barry Island." He hadn't been pulling his weight. All day long he kept sitting down when we should have been standing up, staying in the car when there was walking to do, always looking towards the horizon with sad distant eyes.

I wanted to ask why he couldn't stay, but it was none of my

business, like talking about stepparents. I choose to be on the outside and no one owed me anything.

"How about you? Are you enjoying it here?" he asked, and I nodded. It had started to rain again. I had been holding my coat in my arms, trying to keep up with him, rather than wait to put it on. I struggled with it and my arms the moment we left the coffee shop. Robin waited a few seconds then carried on walking. It was one of the things that I admired about him, the way that he could match my pace. Drizzle was being wrung out of the intense evening like hot lemon towels in restaurants. Where the rain ran, it left brief channels of fresh air, that we could breathe in more easily. We walked briskly.

"If you're enjoying the course, I guess…" he started.

We crossed the road in silence. I was trying to think of how to respond. I glanced over at the dome of the bus station we were nearing. I sensed amongst the lights of the city traffic – brake lights, traffic lights, headlights – all falling upon us that Robin was slowing a little.

He mumbled something ahead of him. He was looking at the floor just ahead of us. It could have been anything, and then quite clearly he added, "I guess you have to stay. No point not to, really," as if he was telling himself.

And even though he was telling me and not asking me if I would come with him, I knew I should have turned to him then. I should have told him I understood him and that I was him and why weren't we together sharing this experience, trusting and understanding.

But I didn't. We walked farther towards the bus depot. His comment hung over us.

I should have stopped. We were already slowing, quite a bit now. I wondered if Robin had lost a little certainty in where we were going. He turned to look at me. "You've gone quiet," he whispered almost reproachfully.

We were looking at each other. I should have asked him what he meant, I should have asked where he was going and, actually, I should have kissed him. How would I have done that? I should have lifted my fingertips to his lips and brushed them gently, traced the shape of them so that I would have been committed to the act without barging ahead.

And it would be magic.

I should have tried to make Robin happy. How did I even know that I could? But I knew that I wanted to. We had slowed. The persistent midlands traffic was throwing a confusion of lights across the road, indicating, braking, headlights, green lights. The bus garage was just a few yards away and Robin was looking at me. But it was the making him happy that stopped me.

But, well, you know. I'm Bernie, the storyteller with the flat bouncy shoes. What possessed me to think I had the power? I knew Robin and his stories of the people he cared about in Africa and the enlightenment they brought to him, a plateau of self-discovery. I just had no gift of happiness. I couldn't live up to him. I was just the storyteller.

And it let me stay adrift. "Just tired," I said. "Thinking about going home." I broke our pace. I walked faster. We had briefly become almost stationary. Robin matched me. I knew he had noticed a change, but he fell in line. Somehow my breath seemed to catch in my throat.

Robin had found his voice again. It wasn't pathways this time, it was the incompetence of the transport system, which seemed a little unfair to me but I didn't point it out. I preferred watching him gabble. "You take the one-o-five?" I asked as we reached the huge map on the kerb and stared for a few moments at the route, Robin doing a fairly good impression of not having a clue what number he was.

He nodded finally. "I'll come to your stop if you want. Wouldn't like to hear of you being mugged or anything."

I laughed at him. He followed me. He hadn't long to wait, the bus was already peeking over the hill. I waited at the window, to say goodbye to him, smiling at him, his aimless chatter. As the bus drew up, he managed to push a peck on the cheek through my defences, he managed to grab my eyes for a second, and he grabbed my arm for a second. He gave it a reassuring squeeze like he was letting me be free.

"Let me take something," Dad had said at the ticket barriers that time I returned from university, after Eleanor, but before Freddie. I couldn't decide what to offer him. The suitcase was the first thing I let go of and he picked it up. I saw the glance at my unwashed hair and observed Dad's decision not to mention it.

Back then, it seemed like I'd been left home for an age, but it had just been eighteen months.

"How was your journey?" It was crowded. The conversation was reserved and perhaps he wasn't going to ask me why I came because he was trying not to make it sound as if I wasn't always welcome there. Ask me why I came, I thought as we neared the car.

We piled the car boot with the luggage. I watched him remove the crook lock and pass it to me so that I could put it on the back seat. "So how is that grant stretching?" Was he fishing? I watched as he negotiated that difficult junction, much smaller than I remembered it. I watched him try not to ask me what was

35

wrong, why I was coming home suddenly during my second year of university. We passed onto the wide straight road and I felt him tense at the continued silence. "I was speaking to Cathy's mum the other day. Apparently, Cathy had to take out a loan to pay the hall fees."

He thought it was the debt. He was right, that huge overwhelming debt that I was defaulting on, big time. And I hadn't informed all the right people at the right time.

"It's not money, Dad," I said and knew that the conversation had reached a new point when I had admitted there was something. But he was going to have to read between the lines. He was going to have to work out that I just couldn't see the point in it anymore.

How could I have done that? Betrayed Dad so easily. Where had I gone wrong? Not trying hard enough; evasive phone calls. I knew. I could see all that debt; all that work all of the time: all that money and effort that Dad had thrown into me to say that Bernie was going to be happy. Whatever else had happened, he had no other cause to fight. And I was returning to say that I had failed, not my exams, not in money management, but in my ability to wake up in the morning and want to get up, or even not notice that there's no point in getting up.

Dad's twenty-year project had failed, and I had to lie about it, but I couldn't even remember how to smile anymore, and I still hadn't answered Dad's question.

I also knew I didn't have to. Dad's questions were so obviously hitting and bouncing off the great black box around my head. Surely that was a state he had known too. That gave me a small relief, that even if he had been in this place too, his recent new dates with the Canadian woman might have changed his path for the better. At this point, I'd only met her the once.

We were speeding along a small, hedged road. Dad had to concentrate. I could hear the concentration in the silence. And I was looking ahead to warn of hazards he might not have seen, so I didn't have to look at him.

It meant that I never knew if he was crying when the way he breathed and moved the car felt strange, when he started to say, "Bernie, is it Eleanor?" from a dry throat. "Because if it's Eleanor, I…"

I didn't want to know what he was about to say. To this day, I never wanted to know if my dad considered giving up his girlfriend for me, escalating that debt. To this day, I never wanted to know if Dad couldn't give up Eleanor for me. "Of course it's not Eleanor. That's a good thing."

If he didn't believe me, he was too relieved to show it.

It had been the beginning of the sealing. The engagement was announced within the week, and if I had felt isolated by the new relationship, then I was relieved by the lifting of that burden. That Dad finally had other projects, more immediate to him, and my debt would be forgotten. I was free to be unhappy.

And somehow, being free to be unhappy was what had lifted me out of that inexplicable lull and I could pretend that visit had never happened.

Chapter 6

I was staying at Dad's when I next heard from Robin.
Dad had invited me formally, sounding like he finally
understood I would only be visiting, and it was easy
enough to accept. And then Robin phoned, telling me that
he was in the area, and we should meet. His voice in my family
house felt too close to home and the daydreams I had locked
up safely away from Warwickshire.

It was out of season. The ice-cream parlour we had agreed
to meet outside was closed. The paint on the wooden shutters

was peeling off. Handwritten-style lettering indicated that fine Devonshire ice cream would otherwise be available at a third of the price of my daily commute.

He wasn't there when I arrived. I zipped up my leather jacket and glowered at the beach to my left. I touched the stone wall to see if it was dry enough to sit on and found that it wasn't. The tide was in. The colour of the sea was a muddy blue.

"Glad I forgot my swimming trunks," I heard suddenly. Robin had come from the other side of the ice-cream parlour. He kissed my cheek, or more accurately, kissed the line of my forehead, and it was neither romantic nor platonic. Cold, amongst the hair flying about the place.

"So where are you staying?" I asked as we walked together, as always just walking with no intention of where we were going to end up. I was confused that he had come this far from London.

"An old friend's floor on a scruffy lilo that makes me wake up thinking I've fallen asleep in the sea." Robin has adrift feelings too, then. We stared out at a rocking sailing boat. "I'm here looking for a couple of sponsors."

I turned to him. "You're so infuriating."

"Am I?"

"Sponsors for what? What is this mysterious project?"

"You never asked."

I hadn't, though I had been desperate to know. Somehow it had felt like it was none of my business. It would have been a crossing of our lives. I didn't belong in his story.

He smiled as if to say, see, I have the upper hand after all. "I have contacts here. It's just taking a visit to convince them that they do want to help."

"Oh, tell me."

39

"It's not that exciting. Well, it doesn't sound exciting. I'm excited by it."

"Come on."

We walked a little further along the promenade. I could see he needed the paces to put his words together, tell me about something big. "When you're in one place, the old world starts becoming 'other worldly'. I started to remember scenes of places I've been in Africa, and they started making stories. Then I started to picture the stories..."

"Okay..." I prompted.

"I want to make, bring something unliving to life. I want someone to understand about the taste of thick tej and pollo wot." He frowns. "This is going to sound so strange. I started to picture all the images forming a huge mosaic, incorporating spirals and mirrors of other lives. It keeps blossoming in my head. I was scared that if I don't make it soon, it will run out of my head, perhaps into someone else's. I have the rest of my life to be boring in."

We started climbing down the wall that slanted from the road to the sand while I thought about his mosaic. "The studying bored you?"

He gave me a sidelong glance. "You knew I didn't fit in there."

"We never talked about it."

"But you knew." And it was strange to hear the understanding between us finally expressed in words. I remembered his affinity with the elements, and the patterns he would leave behind on the shoreline.

"What are you going to live on?"

A smile burst from his face. "This is what I mean. These practicalities..."

"It's serious..."

40

"And I'm joking. I'm not entirely mad." He glanced briefly down, still beaming but embarrassed. "I won a commission – large urban redevelopment in London."

I turned to him, impressed. "You kept that quiet."

He smiled shyly. "There was an ad, in a paper."

We had reached the bottom of the steps. I always forgot the feeling of hearing the waves against the shingle. I had every intention of leaving the old world behind me, but that sound always made me smile.

"The mosaic, it's buzzing. It's running away. It's linked to this amazing bar in London, Zero Bar, which is tiny, but you can get lost in, like a maze of mirrors."

The sky was slate grey like the wall we sat beneath. There was the odd blue patch, but not in the right place for the sun.

The base of the slanting wall was a yard from the water's edge, but the sand was dry. "Is this as far as the water comes?"

"It can reach halfway up the walls." I had been thinking of the mosaic buzzing in Robin's head. "I miss walking along here in the cold wind and hearing the sea when the pub's close; eating fish and chips when it's too dark to see the water, just the fairy lights along the road and the blackness over the sea."

"That sounds good." He tried to look behind us at the shops, but the wall was too high. "We should do that tonight."

"We should." I thought, I should offer to put him up at Dad's, but he would bounce into my locked-up dreams, he would see Eleanor and Dad and know me too well, question why I needed to escape this life.

Seagulls screeched across the water. "Is it going okay here?" he asked gently. "Whenever you come back from here, you seem…" He paused and I remembered coming back to him, determined not to become involved in him. "…different"

"It's okay." I pause, wondering if it's safe to add more. "My dad wants me to stay here." I run my fingers through the pebbles. "Everyone wants me to be in their places, their ideals."

I realised suddenly that I'd woken up the time he had asked me to join him in London. He didn't pretend I hadn't touched a nerve. He squeezed my arm. When I said nothing, he asked, "So where do you want to be?"

Adrift. "Wherever no one wants me to be."

He laughed. I supposed it was a kind of joke. I tried to see his face as I turned to check the traffic as we crossed the road. He saw me looking and smiled vaguely.

"What about *your* parents, anyway?"

He paused briefly in his stride. "Oh, my mum's great. I mean, I suppose she's a housewife but she's really witty and clever."

"And?" I said, using Robin's own tone.

"And my dad's, well, he does everything, job-wise that is. Sometimes he's about and sometimes he isn't." He stared at the water. "We don't get on that well."

"Why not?"

"I don't know. Different worries. Different priorities."

"If he does a lot of other things, he must be a lot like you."

He shook his head. "No. I don't know. He keeps telling me to stick at things. He was married at my age."

"Weren't all of our parents?"

"Yeah, I suppose. But he's much more concerned about how much money you have, rather than how you earned it. Not that he was always winning at that game. Life was up and down. He'd invest in good projects and then in bad, make friends with the right people and then with the wrong."

"You make him sound like the Great Gatsby."

"Yes. He could be Gatsby. I'd like it that way. He didn't have any children, did he?"

I laughed. "You can't hate him that much."

"I can." He deposited dried seaweed on my stomach. I flicked it off in his direction. "I don't hate him. There's just very little to be said between us anymore."

The magician and his father. Men and their fathers. Men and their sons. It reminded me that Robin's son would not get on with Robin. It reminded me of the awkwardness of human relationships. I stood up. "Don't expect cucumber and mint in your Pimms at this pub," I told him.

II

Part Two

Chapter 7

The London Eye, Copyright https://alexmorrall.com

I went to London when I graduated, just like everybody else. I had every excuse to be there that had nothing to do with Robin. It dazzled me, as did the hundreds of thousands of people who held their breath, putting their heads down, masked with sleep and newspapers, and sank down by escalator into the sub-world as the guard shouted instructions into their hypnosis. What a world to be able to be alone in: sounds and myriads of cultures that would let me live alone.

Robin mocked me for saying I liked the tube. "Did you know there are dragons living in the underground? The trains have to keep stopping in the tunnel to let them through. And," he said the word with significance, "from two o'clock to four o'clock when even the most self-respecting criminals have gone to bed, the tube drivers race in the tunnels. Particularly on the Northern Line. They give the Bank branch a head start at Kennington and see who gets to Camden first."

He'd become chattier the longer he'd been back from Africa and we'd met for lunch when I came to check out accommodation, ending with an offer to point out the right routes to some of the properties on my list. He had a year's experience in the city ahead of me, time to find his feet, too, as he worked strange hours on piecing together his mosaic. I'd seen the photos as he went. Some I recognised from earlier descriptions of his gap year. How did the hundreds of subtly different yellow glass shards show so well the intense city daylight of an equatorial vista? Hills were created in coalescing bottle tops, with roads of jade-coloured high-rise buildings and shabby roadside shops, in broken tiles. Smaller tiles marked out counters of bags and cigarettes open onto the road. It was peppered with blue and white taxis. "Lardas," said Robin, but he didn't explain.

We zipped through Bond Street tube station. "What's this job, again?" he yelled over the rush of the rails as we were rattled around, gripping the hold rails.

"They're a bunch of lawyers, do research or find loopholes for things. It's kind of hard to explain. They're putting me on 'inheritances' first. No idea what that means, but the first folder they gave me reminded me of you... it said: Mr Tadesse from Ethiopia."

"Strange work for a geography graduate."

"So, a mosaicist is the right job for a geography grad?"

"Nah, I'm a geography dropout. I'm following a well-trodden path of mosaicists."

"That famous career path."

"You haven't told your dad, have you?"

"It seemed the wrong time." I hesitate, finding something to change the subject. "On the subject of dads... Did I see your dad in the local paper today?" The unusual surname – Hawk – had caught my eye, but when I saw Jonathan Hawk's face, I knew there had to be a connection. "Running as a local counsellor."

Robin shrugged, and there was a shiver of that old awkwardness when either of us ever talked about our families like there was something too close about them. "Is that so he can give you more urban art commissions?"

And he only slightly smiled as the loudspeaker announced Liverpool Street. I looked tentatively at Robin who gave me a reassuring nod through the sardines of passengers, and we emerged in Liverpool Street station at the top of a maze of underground steps. I was hit by the vastness from floor to ceiling, an iron-gridded glass ceiling. Every inch buzzed with people on the escalators, the balconies, the platforms, in the shops. I stared hard at the signs indicating directions and gradually found my way. The train boards flickered, one after the other, with new train details, like swiftly dealt cards. Crowds of people moved in response and my heart rose to the excitement. I had become like a flake of snow, independent in my structure, hidden in the flurry.

"Is that where you're headed?" He pointed up at one of the departure boards and I checked the unknown name against my list and nodded. "Got to be careful going that way. Stay on a train for more than five minutes, and you end up in Essex."

"Where're you going from here?"

He smiled quietly. "Meeting someone who liked my work."

"That's a bit random."

He nodded. "I know. I'll let you know if anything comes of it. They're house hunting too, so I'll be sure to tell them of what you've learned about good areas. Good networking," he added with a wrinkle of his nose.

I laughed at the thought of Robin getting out of his head enough to network. So did he.

The estate agents had viewed me curiously to start with. I was too young, they seemed to imply, either to choose to or afford to live alone. But as soon as they registered that I was a cash buyer, an advantage of my grandmother's small inheritance, professionalism took over.

I found my train with a spring of positivity, thrilled at the independence to be found here. I could get lost in a crowd and be as free of clutter as I was becoming of people. Having loosed myself of one family, one dependency, I could clear out the rest as well.

It made for a tiring day, wandering alone between Victorian conversions and flats above shops. On my third property of the day, I noticed another girl get off the same train as me, and despite the relatively quiet streets, we seemed to be going in the same direction. She was dressed in a sharp trouser suit – royal blue and petite. We arrived at the door with a row of tatty intercoms together. As she came closer, I realised that the suit had given the impression of someone much older than she was. She was my sort of age.

"We're viewing the same property, then," she said to me as we arrived, and raised her eyebrows as I leaned forward to press the relevant buzzer. Close up, I saw her eyes were red, and there was possibly the residue of tears on her cheeks. I didn't have to comment, as we were buzzed in at that moment. "The first floor, wasn't it?" said the girl, already on the stairs. I wondered if she was racing me, as if the first of us to get through the door would be the first to get to bid on the flat, or if she was trying to hide the evidence of tears on her face, but she held the door open at the top of the stairs for me, smiling.

Away from the stairs, we found a waiting estate agent with the door open. He led us in. "Gemma, and Bernie, right?" he muttered from his notes and we both said yes at the same time. "Well don't mind me, feel free to have a proper hunt around."

We walked awkwardly into the front room, unsure as to how to size up a property even if we'd been alone. It was mostly white, clearly without a current occupant. It had probably been other things than white until recently. The wallpaper, for example, looked like it had been an embossed eighties pattern, now painted white, and the fireplace, boarded up, was quite white now too. Like the metal window frames, and the built-in shelving. I looked over at the girl, Gemma, to make eye contact a couple of times, but she didn't respond, opening a built-in cupboard to peer into. From the open door, I could see the estate agent making notes from his phone onto paper on the kitchen counter. "Not much, is it?" I risked.

She winced without looking at me. "The smell of damp can't be healthy."

I nodded. "I know." I turned back onto the mosaiced floor of the hallway. The estate agent was now chatting on his phone. It sounded like a private call. "Sorry to ask, but are you okay?"

This time she looked at me as if there was no point pretending if she was that obvious. "I just…" she looked at me again and sighed. "House hunting on my own, on my holiday time from my brand new PR job where they still think I'm just a useless skiver. This just wasn't supposed to happen, and…" she paused, as if unsure that she should share the next part to a house-hunt competitor, "…I just have no idea how I'm going to afford this."

She wandered into the bedroom as if she had said too much, and stared, nose pointing to each of the four corners of the ceiling, some pretence at checking out the state of the flat.

I followed her through and sat on the only remaining item of furniture – a plastic-wrapped mattress on a pine bed. Opposite me, two tall windows were looking out onto the road. I winced up at her from the bed. "Sorry. What went wrong?"

"I fell out with the friends I was supposed to be moving in with."

"Okay."

"Like really big time." I don't know why, but the slang slightly jarred with her immaculate appearance and sleekly cut hair. "I came home from work and found my stuff on the front yard." Her voice caught again.

"Oh, wow. What was their problem?"

"They thought I was snooty because I'm never around. It's my job you see. I'm supposed to be in PR, but they get me doing everything… It not that it's not fun stuff. I was researching a location for one of their clients to use as a film set."

Just then, we heard the estate agent stirring, and remembered where we were. He came to the door with a frown on his face to find us sitting on the bed. He looked at his heavy silver watch with exaggerated significance. Part of me really wanted to ignore him and carry on chatting, but 'Gemma' obediently stood as if we were naughty school kids. I was willing her not to apologise. She managed at least not to do that.

In the hallway, with the smell of fresh paint and damp mixed together, the estate agent ushered us towards the front door. "Right, well…" This was the part when they would normally say they would be in touch, but we were all aware that we had not seen the kitchen and no one in their right state of mind would buy a flat without having seen the kitchen.

"I think we annoyed him," she said, smiling as we stood back on the weeded pathway. It had felt a little rude to just part company at the front door.

I shrugged. I'd already seen enough of them let their egos trip up a sale. "The bathroom didn't smell of rot, I suppose."

"It's all we're going to get if we want our independence."

I shivered at the alternative. "I hate sharing." She looked downcast again, and I realised I had hit a nerve. I felt sorry. She was lost and alone, but she was different from me. She wasn't battling to stay alone. "Do you want to grab a drink?"

Chapter 8

Got to tell you something about Robin. We've spoken again. I made the effort to call him, let him know about a class reunion but he was in the middle of something, walking between a meeting, could give me five minutes of his breathless time.

It's just a suspicion, but it's rippling clearer in my head, day by day. Robin, he's radiant. He's creating again.

All this networking, this chatting with PR, it's got its buzz when it starts, but it's not what Robin is, my magician, it's not what Robin is. It's hibernation at the end of the day.

I can see him, hoarding stories like acorns, letting some of them slip into oak trees. He's doing what his long, long legs were meant to lead to. There's a new idea in there, in his head, spilling into conversations, scribbled notes, photographs; if I know Robin, it will be something completely different.

His mosaic next to Zero Bar is going to be like ash in comparison to his new sparks. I daydream about the cogs, the shafts, the furnace rocking into life with that first heavy definite thump, an ache of life and another thump, the next quicker. Red-hot coals and a swarm of salsa-ing sparks.

I peered harder into his world. All the beautiful things I knew about the labyrinth, the city, his discoveries, were all ingrained in his first mosaic. Where did he find his energies from? Not these. He must see how everything moves, from journeys overseas; shifts in relationships to ants scurrying underneath the everyday, electrons soaring around nuclei, to find so much dynamism all of the time, a Prussian doll of dynamisms. Robin's found all the layers and is about to start adding them together. Where from? Where from?

Has Robin fallen in love? No. Well, maybe. His other muses have long flown; the space is there waiting for 'the one'. It could explain his awakening, ease of accomplishment.

"So, what's going on in your life at the moment?" I ask him down the phone.

"Oh, everything. We must catch up sometime. Sorry I can't make the reunion." There is the sound of a swinging door. "Look, Berns, I've got to go. I'll call you back." Robin soars off.

A bit later, he sent me a text. "This amazing thing has happened with my mosaic – it's going to be part of something big. I'll explain soon."

And I envied him a little as I left my lonely flat to meet up with Gemma from the flat-hunt day.

Gemma and I had casually stayed in touch and would meet for the odd drink in the very same pub we'd chosen on the day we'd met. She seemed to need adopting, but I had been reluctant to impose my help on her, knowing I would have hated that from someone else.

We clicked over the similarities of our jobs. For me, 'being put on inheritances' turned out to mean identifying unclaimed estates and researching genealogies to find their beneficiaries. My storyteller knack paid off. I pieced together the stories of the family trees and left-over documents. I could work out where the beneficiaries' lives had led them so that my employer could contact them and arrange further investigation 'for a fee'. As soon as they'd worked out they could trust me, they'd throw me a dusty file, tell me the objective, and then leave me to it.

Both Gemma and I were lost in the silent isolation of pursuing stories for our bosses. For me, the detective work of uncovering family trees and rifts and secret families; for Gemma, the researching locations for film sets, sent out with nothing but a script and the streets of London.

"It's a cool job," I'd reassured her.

"That's what my housemates said, that I think I'm too cool for them. I'm not even cool." It was almost funny to see her tiny frame so exasperated, but I felt for her. "I'm good at it because I'm diligent, which is the opposite of cool, and anyway I joined the company to do PR."

I knew silence was the best way to let her feel calm again. After a while she'd speak. "And it's not noble like yours. All those thank you letters you get."

For all the silence of my new life, it was true I'd receive letters and emails of thanks from suddenly wealthy recipients who'd previously had no idea what affluence was coming their way. "But I can't really help people, you know. Not people who really need help. Some of them think that we're a private detective agency."

"What do you mean?'

"They assume we can help with other stuff after we've been in touch. And of course, having received inheritances, they now have the money to pay for it." I told her about the man who'd been pressing on my conscience, Mr Tadesse, who had been left a sum of money by an older friend, a mentor who'd lost touch when Mr Tadesse had returned to his parents' home country to 'make a difference' as a medic. "This huge long handwritten letter of thanks, also telling me that his son was killed in a shoddily built school from a British charity and could we look into it, because he was sure that someone was accountable?"

"What did you do?"

"I wrote to explain we're not an investigations firm. We were set up to make money in the most reliable and mundane way we knew how, but he replied with details of the British charity behind the building, enclosing glossy leaflets of 'Education Sinclair', and building plans that meant nothing to me. I couldn't help. I just felt so hopeless."

"Bernie, private investigator," Gemma announced. "I can see you being just like a character from a Raymond Chandler. You even have that bitter dry sense of humour."

Bitter? I don't know how to take the word, and recoil slightly.

Gemma clocks my reaction. "I just mean, I don't know reconciled to, I don't know, isolation, not expecting anything from anyone... I'm digging a hole here..."

Did she mean my inability to help Mr Tadesse? Maybe his letter just filled me with sadness because Mr Tadesse was the son of Ethiopian refugees who came here in the seventies and I recognised the reference to the country that Robin had spent so much time in.

"I'm not isolated. I'm going to a reunion of my old post-grad colleagues on Saturday." I pause for a minute, thinking of Gemma's isolation. "Just for a meal but you could come actually, if you wanted?"

She gives a surprising quick smile, and whispers, "Actually, I'm going on a date." She quickly suppresses the smile. "I met him through work just before you and I became friends, but I don't want to get too excited. It all seems too good to be true at the moment."

Chapter 9

There hadn't been many of us on the post-grad. Neil, Sophie and her boyfriend Luke, Shelley, a South African who never really spoke to the rest of us, Mark and Noel. Robin had left after the first two months. It was unlikely Shelley's contact details would be known by anyone and Mark and Noel were out of the country. So just the four of us once I'd ascertained that Robin couldn't make it. Neil had arranged the evening, having some sense of social cohesion that the rest of us failed to muster.

Luke slid into the seat next to me while I was talking to Sophie. I cringed as he did so having quickly gathered when I met him that Luke was the sort of person who gained attention by putting everyone else down. He had a knack for it, seemingly smelling someone's weakness and knowing just enough to win the conversation. His move next to me put me on instant alert.

He'd made an effort tonight, smelling of shampoo and his blond hair spiked into a fountain at the front of his head like he'd just come out of an eighties hairdresser.

"You could have ordered a drink for me," he muttered at looking at the dark wood table full of wines and waters. A waiter was conveniently walking past as he said it and stopped politely, pen in hand as Luke made the order, taking surreptitious glances in our direction. He was flooding the table, more overpowering than the incense with the fact that he had something to say. "Hello, darling. How are you?" He grinned and squeezed my shoulder. I glowered at him for a few seconds. I could be rude about his hair, but he'd think I was joking. I've come to realise that any politeness to Luke is taken as a come on.

"Your girlfriend was just telling me about her job interview." I nodded at Sophie. Luke leaned back in his chair.

"Oh, I've heard all of this already. Mean, weren't they? Where's this belly dancer we were promised?" He had one hand behind the back of his head, leaning against the wood panelling. Luke has a series of model poses that he performs when he wants to get looked at. Why doesn't Sophie see it? He only leaves pause enough to establish an end to that conversation. "I heard something very interesting today."

Subtlety never was Luke's strong point. And I guessed at that moment what he was about to say; I knew it then. I only had one weakness. I wasn't going to ask, though. I was just going to carry on staring at the red curtains and the silver plates of pita and humous going to other people's tables, thinking about poor Sophie's job interview. I didn't gain much ground by not asking. Luke's too thick to get it. He ploughed on. "Robin's got a new girlfriend."

Just because I expected it, didn't mean I didn't catch my breath. I raised my eyebrows in response, aware that the whole table was looking at me. "Really, who's that?"

"Something to do with work." Another mosaicist, then. Are there many of those? "I met her. She's really nice. She's called, oh, I can't remember her name."

"Where did you meet her?"

"I met Robin for a quick drink after work when one of my clients took me his way and she was with him."

I couldn't think of anything to say. My cheeks were burning. I needed the toilet but thought it would look stupid to go then. "His dad was running for local counsellor in one of the boroughs; I saw it in the newspaper recently. Don't know what happened, though."

He said nothing and pulled a mean smile so I changed tack.

"Sophie was just saying how good the menu was here. Have you been before, Luke?"

He looked at me for a few seconds longer, sipping his newly arrived lager through his grin. "You've come over all polite."

I smiled nervously, but Sophie eventually spoke for him. "He hasn't been here before. The service is great, as well as the food. The starter feels like a main course and you get Turkish delight and baklava at the end."

I picked up the menu from the centre of the table and stared into it. Luke leaned forward making me jump. His arm slid around my waist and he looked at me intently. "Cheer up, Bernie. You really have to lighten up you know."

I couldn't work out how I had given so much away.

After Turkish delight and baklava, we got up and ambled through paying the bill, ambled towards Waterloo, and I stopped while the others walked on. And the thing that made me choke in the dust and diesel of Waterloo Bridge, was not Luke's presumption that he knew my close friend better than me, nor the hurt of knowing that Robin was seeing someone. It was the possibility that Luke knew how much the news would affect me, the possibility of Luke knowing how I felt about Robin, which made the feeling of it worse.

I wanted to merge with the paving, dissolve into Waterloo Bridge where I would be long forgotten and no one would give time to knowing or gossiping about who I really was.

I felt a pair of hands against my shoulders and I hoped beyond hope that they weren't Luke's, that he had not seen my delayed reaction. But as another cheek neared mine, I realised, it was Neil. "It's okay, Bernie. It's okay," he said to the patch of the floor I was staring at.

Leave me alone, I thought. But I was being straightened by Neil's grip on my shoulders. He wasn't checking my pulse or asking me if I was okay. He was telling me I was okay. I found myself staring out over the Thames, the lights of the night caught in its ripples.

Neil was giving me a concerned look. "I think I tripped, lost my balance," I muttered not meeting his eye

He nodded. "I know." He held my arm in his hand. A slow-walking couple walked past us, stopping their conversation while we were near. After they passed, his hand slid down to my fingers and we held hands. "I think the night isn't over, yet,

Bernie," he told me and I didn't argue as he turned me around to face Aldwych again.

We neared the whitened buildings in the orange light. Beetles of cabs and two limos were greying up the air and crowding out the traffic lights so that we couldn't cross the road. "Looks like a show's just finished," Neil said.

"Hey, where are you two going?" It was Luke's voice from somewhere behind us. I had gotten confused about where everybody was. The tone suggested that he hadn't seen my confusion.

I didn't turn, suspecting that my face would give everything away. Neil turned. "Bernie's left her jacket in the bar. We'll catch up with you." I heard no response, imagined they were shrugging. Why did Neil lie?

I didn't wonder where we were going, just glad of the comfort of Neil's height next to me and the security of his hand. I knew that he filled a Robin-shaped proximity, but only vaguely. I was tired, worn out, trying to find excuses for my earlier distance. "So, Bernie," he began, "London is here. Where shall we start?"

Just occasionally, London offers so many choices that not one place lives up to the idea of being able to go anywhere. Neil seemed to guess from my silence that I didn't want the burden of decision making. He steered me to a windowed door. Frosted glass with an imprinted art deco border was held in ageing blond wood. I briefly caught a name. Something like, 'The Deer Leap', something meaningless and forgettable. The door was opening onto crowds and crowds.

We fought to the bar where he bought me a glass of wine. He handed it to me, palm over the top and I took it, cradling it in two hands, staring at the misty glassiness. After our large meal and drinks, the thought of the wine was like poison. It made me retch to look at it. He put an elbow on the bar and lifted his pint, asked how work was, and I told him a bit about it, a bit about some sad letters I'd been receiving at work from a Mr Tadesse who had lost his son in a collapsed school overseas, and how the more he wrote to me, the more I could see that there must have been foul play. My voice ran out of energy.

I felt suddenly self-conscious about the sad story that had suddenly come to mind, recollecting the moment that had brought us both here and stared for a few moments at the bar, swallowing. He said nothing either.

"I just lost my balance back there," I said weakly. I was still shaking slightly, excuses for my behaviour cramping out my mind.

I glanced up at him. He wasn't looking at me, his eyes unfocussed towards the bottles at the back of the bar. This time, he didn't say that he knew. He just nodded very slightly and I knew for definite then, that he was not here to listen about Robin, to offer a shoulder to cry on.

Relief. How do you describe crying over what you distinctly decided you didn't want, making Neil believe that it was humiliation, not so much loss that had hurt me?

Then recognition of why I was there.

He sipped from his drink again and I realised I had not drunk mine. I couldn't think of anything to say and decided, Neil had bought me here so he could handle the conversation.

"We've only got a quarter of an hour." He indicated a white clock face above my head. "Think there's someone interesting playing at Smolenski's."

"Really? Who?"

He shook his head, laughing at the bar. "Don't know. Just thought, I could imagine you hanging out there."

My turn to nod quietly.

"Luke's just great, isn't he?"

"No."

He laughed again. "Why does Sophie always have to bring him?"

"I thought about not coming when I realised he'd be there."

He looked up sharply. "I'm glad that you did," he said, slightly crimson. I could see that he was struggling to find a compliment. Wondered if I should help him out. "I like your company," was what he eventually came up with. My guess was Neil didn't do this often. Compliments are meant to be physical so that everybody knows where they're headed. But he touched my arm at the same time and Neil doesn't normally do stuff like that with friends. "Drink up," he added.

I stared more at the glass and tried sipping a little. Another good way of avoiding conversation. It struck me then that I wasn't holding on all that redundantly because I was worried about offending Neil. Partially, I wanted a distraction from Robin, and I was curious to see exactly how much flattery I was going to get here, to see if I was going to enjoy this.

A bell rang throughout the pub, deafening the thought out of my head. The last orders bell. "See what I mean about drinking up?"

I did so as politely as possible, just to clear the glass of the maddening liquid. He drained his lager.

When I pushed my glass next to his, there was still an inch or so of wine in there, and a mouthful still in my mouth that I swallowed awkwardly. I knew I was frowning. "Smolenski's then," I said and Neil smiled. He slipped an arm around my waist.

"Definitely."

It was awkward moving interlinked through a crowded pub and we clattered clumsily past the warmth of noise, out of the front steps and onto the road. I'm sure, this patch of London was dirtier by night, lit by orange lights instead of a grey sky. Closed shops were steel cages rather than homes of white light, and the graffiti on the shutters becomes more obvious. We passed dark corners of homeless, gathered teenagers and just darkness. Then a couple of metres further down the road, Neil reached with his other hand to my arm and put his face close to mine.

I don't normally do things like this, I reminded myself again. I was not enjoying the experience because I hadn't learned to enjoy it. I studied Neil's features while he studied mine and I wondered what it was that made him so evidently good looking but still unattractive to me. His breath smelt of lager. That at least reminded me of Robin. "Bernie," Neil eventually said. I knew I would return whatever he tried, but afterwards, I would leave, clumsily, using that clumsiness as the excuse. "You don't really want this do you?" I put a hand on his shoulder and levered my face away from his. I shook my head. I couldn't meet his eye.

"Sorry," I mumbled.

He sighed and moved his arm from my waist. "No problem," he said confidently. There was a silence.

"I suppose I'd better get home," I said. I meant I wished I was at home now, wished I'd gone home when everybody else had, not stranded out here with all the fatigue after a long day in a wakening nightlife that I couldn't swim in.

"Yeah, me too." He shrugged.

What was I supposed to say then? See you later? When I knew I wouldn't. "See you."

"Yeah, see you. Bye."

Chapter 10

I woke to a screeching alarm and staggered out of bed. Dad had left a message on my phone. "Need to chat, love. Call me back." Not at this time of the morning, I suspected, tossing the phone onto the sofa. It looked like he had called while I was out last night. I wandered back to the kitchen. I was up early for my research, trying to piece together a story of an inheritance question, working out what the links could be, and what the threats to any theory would be. The monotony of my new life was incessant. I woke early and thought about work straight away. It was a way of finding a reason for getting up in the mornings

But the quiet job suited me. Being 'left to it' was what I wanted, better than being hounded, than being mothered. The silence was beginning to follow me. It would follow me from the dusty files to my quiet flat and I wasn't quite sure what to do with it. I longed to hear from Robin, but I knew I'd chosen to stay adrift.

And I forgot about Dad's call the following afternoon when I eventually woke up. I ran a hot bath with relaxing oils and played CDs from my pre-university days.

I switched on my kettle amongst the warm woods of the kitchen and filled the teapot with jasmine tea leaves. As soon as the boiling water hit them, the blue china became a ball of relaxing steam. I didn't have to drink the tea.

I had woken to ringing a couple of times in the morning but skated back into sleep before I worked out how to answer it and Dad's message came briefly to mind as I checked the new voicemails. The silence of being alone in the new city hurt me too. I could feel it making me doubt who I was, what I stood for, but I didn't want it to take someone else to take that away from me.

I pressed 'play' on the messages. It was Gemma. "Sorry I keep missing you. I really want to catch up. I want you to meet this new boyfriend I told you about." I felt relieved for her as she chattered about meeting him. I felt relieved for me, the freedom from having to look after her. Then, "His name's Robin."

Of course, there are so many Robins. There are probably even many Robins who Gemma would find in her job of finding locations for film sets. Or maybe there are not. Probably there are not.

I bit down every emotion. I thought of work, of how I loved to chase the patterns of stories and how that made me feel valued. I thought of Mr Tadesse and what on earth I could do for him from here. I felt my adrift persona, my confidence. I quickly texted Gemma. "You've got to bring him to dinner sometime soon."

That weekend I opened the door to the two people who had just buzzed white noise from the intercom throughout the flat and I had buzzed them in without checking that it was them because I knew it would be the couple I had invited to dinner. When I saw Gemma and her boyfriend at my door, I opened my mouth and closed it again. My outlandish guess had turned out to be entirely correct. "So do I get to be best man and bridesmaid?" I asked. Only half of my face managed to smile. Gemma looked confused.

And so here in front of me was Robin, the magician whom I hadn't kissed on the way to the bus depot, or responded to a hand squeeze, because I was just the storyteller who didn't belong in the romantic world. And here was the magician, appropriately wrapped up with a good-hearted heroine. The happy ending was on my doorstep. Robin was in it. I wasn't.

And I had put tea lights out and considered friendly, but not too simple, meals. I chose lasagne, I'm afraid – the old student opt-out – and ice cream. The main course bubbled away in the kitchen, filling the kitchen with a family smell that the room was too small to have. And even though I'm independent, bouncy-shoed Bernie, the scruffy finder of narratives, I had stressed about the food and how the conversation would go.

"Bernie." Robin didn't look surprised. If he hadn't worked it out before this evening, he must have worked it out en route. He would have said, "Oh, I have a friend who lives around here," quite a while back in the journey. He would have wondered if every turning would be the one away from my house, or past it.

After all, that was the relationship he had with Gemma; every time he got closer to her, he took a turning away from me.

And Gemma had heard about Robin from me but I'd never told her the full story. I'd chosen detachment, frozen the comments that would threaten my distance before the names came to my mouth. Had I betrayed her more by loving Robin, or by my silence?

I smiled, led them into my front room and I started bringing glasses in, out of the kitchen with their scratching singing clinks. "How on earth did you two meet?" But of course, I could work that out. The 'big thing' for Robin's mosaic would be featuring in one of those arty films that Gemma was researching. "I've been meaning to get my two friends together for a long time, but you've always insisted on being away at the same time," I called from the kitchen. I meant it, kicking myself for not working out a Gemma and Robin plot before they did. I could have engineered it, sealing myself out of the complications of friendship, sealed up and shelved, leaving me free.

I was pulling the Sauvignon out of the fridge. Chill on my fingers that I let spread to the rest of me. The neck slipped abruptly to my fingers, slamming against the fridge door. The dew on the bottle had proved too hard to hold in the hands that I had told must not shake. I hoped that they hadn't heard the crash. I returned to the front room and filled everyone's glasses, to drown out my love. They sat on my sofa, bemused.

71

Having calmed my hands, I wondered if I was acting too cool.

"How did we all know each other and not get to know about it?" Robin asked. His hand rested near Gemma's, not quite touching. He looked a little drained of the magic right then. I wished I could blame Gemma.

"Funny," agreed Gemma. Yeah, funny. Someone really should laugh around about now. We really should have been laughing. That irrational fear of your guests having nothing to say when they get to your house was becoming a reality. "Actually, thinking about it, the only reason that Bernie and I were visiting the same flat the day we met was because Robin mentioned that was a good area to live."

Of course. My heart sank. This was not so much of a coincidence after all. Robin had told me he'd met someone who was house hunting too and shared my research. There can't have been that many properties to see in the area. We probably saw several of the same places, but only one where our paths crossed.

"We've just come from picking up a copy of Robin's photos," Gemma continued sweetly, conversationally, "from Africa."

"Won't they be too old by now?"

"Not very good at getting films processed," Robin said to a patch of rug near the window. "Forgot I had it actually," he added, looking up, gathering himself. "When you start living somewhere, you stop taking photographs of it."

"Do you want to see them?" asked Gemma.

I would have wanted to see them, used every glossy slip to pull together the picture of Robin in my mind. But I was sitting there, sitting cross-legged in the centre of my round rug, drowning it all out, too chilled to be curious. I must have been frowning.

"You know how boring other people's holiday snaps are, Gem," Robin said for me.

"You ready to eat?" I stood up abruptly. "I've laid out plates in the dining room." They stood up and followed me.

Lasagne landed on each bright white plate, fresh, hot, golden. Now I resented all the warmness I had set up, the lasagne, the night lights. I made them add fresh rocket leaves. As they started to eat, I tried to become less frantic, the food thumping in my stomach. Robin began to relax. He was already forgetting. He had already forgotten. "I think, Bernie, that you've been hiding Gemma and me from each other," he grinned.

Very jolly, jolly, Robin. After all, there was nothing remotely unusual about us all being there like that, was there? I smiled my half-face smile again for him and his, jolly, jolly. I didn't know what to say to that. "Any ideas where the next project is coming from, Robin?"

"Africa again," Gemma told me.

"I got interested in the politics."

"Really?"

He leaned back in his seat. "Did you know that Egypt has planes situated on their border, ready to bomb Ethiopia if they build a dam for the Nile? Ethiopia needs that water."

"Do you believe any story anyone tells you, Robin?" And making that dig was the closest I came to warm that evening.

Gemma's head snapped up at my reaction.

Robin looked at me and smiled. "Only the interesting ones."

I left them in the front room to the sound of strumming and acoustics and went to get the ice cream. I caught a backwards glance at them through the hinges of the door. I could see the back of Gemma's head bobbing as she made some comment to

Robin. I could see Robin's head rise and moved out of the way before he caught my eye. I hoped he wouldn't follow me out. The warmth might thaw me.

I felt intrusive even asking how they met and imagined making up the story from the data. *Gemma and Robin, perhaps during a romantic meal. She's confessed her admiration for his work. And now as the first night light started to shudder, at the end of its wax, the conversation was slower and Robin's fingertips reached for Gem's. He says, "I'm glad..."*

No, no. Not then. Not like that. Try... *after the meal, all of it eaten with flush-cheeked laughter, just before they part at the station. Perhaps they do part. They kissed goodbye and Gemma started walking towards her platform and he reached out to pull her back. "Gem, I wanted to tell you..."*

But what's the point in digging up the detail? I can see the pair are serious. The big grown-up mutual love thing and achieved normality, all the things that don't belong in my life and I had assumed didn't belong in Robin's. Hope that's what they wanted.

I started gathering the spoons. Gemma would one day look at me and wonder why I was not attracted to him. Don't all couples believe that the world wants their other half? Maybe she'd ask me, "Bernie, what was it about Robin that meant that you weren't attracted to him? I mean, you were close, I've realised. And both single. I don't understand."

"Are you coming to this launch thing, the thing that features Robin's mosaic?" I swung around at the voice. Gemma was leaning in my kitchen door frame, her arms folded and she was looking at the ceiling the way she does when she is thinking. She didn't seem to notice my surprise.

More icy fingertips from the frost of the ice-cream carton

that I held too long while I worked out what she had asked me. "Oh, yeah. He always calls it the film that ends with the heroine achieving normality."

Gemma wrinkled her little nose. She thought I was criticising.

"Sounds fun."

She stepped a little closer and lowered her voice. I was aware of him out there swimming in the music. "Do you think his work's any good?" She was asking like she needed the approval herself.

"Yeah, really good." But I could only remember that it was good, not feel it, as I resorted to beliefs I had had before they turned up on my door.

She smiled neatly, apparently contented by my answer. She folded into an envelope of 'happy, everything is perfect,' Gemma.

I started to walk towards the door, but she stopped me again. "He doesn't," she began. She was hovering, her free hand extended slightly in an unfinished gesture.

"He doesn't what?"

"Well, does he irritate you? Do you think I should have fallen for someone else?"

"Robin doesn't irritate me."

"But tonight, you were kind of inclined to laugh at him and I know that he thinks that's friendliness, but sometimes I wonder if it's more than that: that you don't like him." I looked at her for a long time. Gemma really did not know me. Had I meant to be cut that far adrift?

I tried, "I think you have made an excellent choice of boyfriend," and judging from her smile as she turned back towards the door, I'd guess I pulled it off.

They huddled at my front door at half-past midnight, ready to leave as I switched off the kitchen light. Gemma kissed my cheek, tucking a stray hair from her bob over one ear. "That was a lovely evening, Berns. I hope we haven't been too much hard work." She was all rosy-cheeked and happy.

"Not at all. It was good to see you again."

Then Robin, who also kissed my cheek. "Goodnight. It's been," he raised his eyebrows, "unusual."

Since my meal with my old class, the news from Luke and the night with Neil, I had tried to make Robin platonic to me. But it hit me at that moment, after my cool chill act, believing myself that he was no longer a problem, that the shock of seeing him so close, how he always was, having alighted all of this personality to platonicism, sent me reeling to a love too physical that I had to let them quickly out of the house so that I could crush it into shape again.

I had been so proud of hitting this state of unselfishness I thought that I'd never reach. I didn't want to lose it, never tried, leaving my love un-embittered and lingering.

I tried not to think of their story anymore, because making Robin and Gemma's story mine, would mean that I would own it. I would have possession over Gemma and Robin and their love. Every love story is a love triangle of the protagonists and the narrator. No one ever questions it. But I lost that right to intrude after meeting Robin, after coming back from my grandmother's funeral, when I pulled away from the closeness I had imagined so often, or perhaps even before that.

This is for two people, not to be diluted through my perceptions.

I'd left the phone off the hook. There was another call from Dad flashing on the phone. I'd call back later. I had work tomorrow. There was no room for emotion. I went straight to bed and lay stone still, holding my breath until I fell asleep.

Chapter 11

Freddie held a carrot-coloured plastic rabbit in his hand. It squeaked when he squeezed it – in other words, often – with a sound like a baby's hiccup but more pathetic. He dropped it, running towards me, jam around his mouth and I knelt to let him kiss me with his sweet strawberry smell.

"Bunny," he chuckled.

"Bernie," I corrected sternly. "How are you, my little Freddie?" I hugged and tickled him and he giggled uncontrollably.

Eleanor was in the doorway. I smiled up at her. "Bernadette," she nodded.

Yes, that made it home, that awkwardness with Eleanor. I

felt like I was crushed between two planes, trying to be distinct from my family, trying to get away from Robin and Gemma. Anyway, just a visit for the day this time, and I was here for a reason, pulled, or rather pushed to the peace of the raft by the rockings of the past two weeks' events.

From the window, I could see Dad's shadow coming towards the door. How to shut them out, how to shut them out. My mind flapped, trying to be free of the swarming flies of intrusions. All the lines they'd use with me. They'd all be the same as before.

I needed to take out the raft. I needed to remind myself I chose adrift.

"Did you want to visit the fair on the beach this afternoon? I'm taking Freddie straight after lunch," Eleanor asked me as I spooned hot yellow potatoes onto my plate.

"I'm okay. I just came for a rest."

Eleanor looked up from glistening carrots and quickly half-glanced at Dad. "You weren't planning on using your room, were you?"

I'm sure the poor thing meant well, but there are better ways to broach subjects you don't want broached. I didn't want to sound confrontational. "Why's that?" The dull chill of a glass of water was already at my lips.

Eleanor glanced at Dad again. "Just got some stuff in there. We can put it to one side if you want to use the room."

Five bedrooms and two bathrooms in this house and mine was used for clutter.

"You wanted me to take you to your grandma's house this evening, anyway, didn't you?" It was my dad who caught my eye.

79

I carved into my plate, distracted from my room. "As long as it really is on your way. I could drive myself." He'd told me he had a business meeting in town. I wanted to be alone at Grandma's. "I did just want to check out my room, though," I added after a while. My fairy-story volumes.

"No problem, no problem." Freddie burped his lunch down his front in that winning way toddlers have.

The conversation was forgotten by the time I thumped upstairs to find a book to take to Grandma's and I was shocked to find a large number of suitcases all over the floor, open everywhere, like a spilt deck of cards. Musty smell. All of them were empty. The emptiness made me catch my breath. My room looked suddenly bare to see all those contained rectangles of vacancy outlined.

I couldn't bypass them to reach the creaking brick of stories on the shelf on the other side of the room. "Dad," I called, backing out of the door and moving downstairs, my feet negotiating the spiralling steps. "Dad, what's going on?"

But it was Eleanor I found sitting at the bottom of the stairs, her long skirt pulled over her knees, red flowers embossed in red material. "I didn't realise that you were going up there," she said.

"What's going on?" I repeated. "My room is full of suitcases."

She looked at the wall behind me, at a watercolour of the Lake District from before Eleanor's time, from before my time. Her hair was slightly greyer than I had noticed before. "I think it would be easier if your dad explained."

"You're going away somewhere?"

"Yes." She still didn't look at me. I studied the lines and marks on her face, trying to work out someone I had met five, perhaps six times. One broken blood vessel; crinkles where everyone

80

had crinkles; lines deep as folds, deeper than scratches. "Robin," she said abruptly, gathering the lines into a frown.

"Pardon?"

"Your dad mentioned you had a friend, Robin. What became of him?"

I'd mentioned Robin to Dad? I hadn't thought so. It's an odd experience to open your mouth, to pretend that you have words that you are about to say because the situation demands it, but be filled with so much emptiness as, well, as the suitcases in my bedroom. My mouth closed again and I crossed the hallway as if she wasn't there; found my way to the bench on the lawn and sat down there. Then I realised I should have just said, "I'm going outside."

I stared at birds shooting across the sky. When had I been so stupid as to mention Robin? The bench was in the shade of the trees, and with the slight breeze, I was almost cool.

Dad found me outside. He had his car keys in his hand and some casual cloth jacket on. He closed the outside door of the porch and stood there. He didn't join me on the bench. He was learning.

"Was it that Eleanor spoke about Robin or the fact that we're going away?"

"When did I mention Robin?" Why do they keep trying to touch me? Haven't they got enough? Each other, Freddie? What did they want from me?

"You were anxious to get back to him after you came for Grandma's funeral. You mentioned him when we talked on the raft. I wasn't sure but…"

Whatever anyone knows about me, whatever good sentiment they might attribute to me, I cannot believe that they'd expect me to be able to tell them about Robin. What was there to tell?

Somewhere, perhaps, there was a galaxy of Robin – exploding nebulae, black holes, orbital paths, comets, unexplained and undiscovered phenomena – and they expected me to find it and put it into words? "I didn't mean to give away a confidence. It was just a vibe on my part." He could see this was not something I wanted to talk about and knew to walk away at this point, not to pile on the pressure. He walked to the people carrier and opened the doors. After a few moments, I climbed in next to him.

"And about the going away… You never asked me why I have a business meeting so close to your grandma's," he said, turning on the ignition.

I crushed the inclination to mimic his question back to him. "You're selling the house?" The thought hit as the words thumped out.

"Did you expect us to keep it?"

"Of course not. I'd wondered why you'd kept it for so long."

"I've been," he pulled at the steering wheel to take us out of the village and sighed as we fell onto the long main road, "getting used to the idea."

"And where are you going with the money?" What were the suitcases in my room all about?

He frowned. "Eleanor has relatives in Canada; one of them is sick."

"You're spending all that money to stay with relatives?"

"Bernie, we're setting up home there." His voice ran out of steam, then he steered it back to its normal level. "I mean, we're going for a long time. We'll keep here, this house. It's your home."

Freedom and fear rushed into me at the same time. I was being left to live my own life; no one was trying to fit me into theirs anywhere. This was what I wanted, wasn't it?

"I know I should have told you earlier, but you're so…" I could feel him searching for words, "untraceable."

"Untraceable?"

"You're always out when I call."

"I have voicemail."

"I left messages."

Oh, yes. He had. I'd forgotten. "Bernie, call me back, need to talk." He was my dad. We talked whenever. That's why I hadn't replied.

"Eleanor hasn't settled so well."

I never thought of it before, but the houses – Dad's and Grandma's – they reeked of Dad and me and solitude, acres of space and heritage to represent a pre-Eleanor life. Perhaps to Eleanor, there was more of my mother there than there ever had been to me.

"How long before Freddie goes to nursery?"

He didn't answer.

"I'm just trying to gather a picture. I don't mind what you say." I stopped. Did that sound callous?

"Yeah. Freddie's schooling makes a difference to how permanent any move would be, but we haven't made a decision yet."

I pulled open the glove compartment and rummaged around. There was always a CD in the glove compartment. Sure enough, I found it, secured in half a CD case and unidentifiable from its picture. I scraped it out and put it into the player. The car became full of *Jumping Jack Flash*.

An hour or so later, I opened my eyes to the crackle of gravel as we pulled onto the drive.

"Asleep?" he asked.

I shook my head. "Just bored of looking at the road." I clicked open the door the moment he pulled on the handbrake. "How are you for time?"

He bobbed his head to the clock on the dashboard. "Cutting it fine." He turned to me. "Just you be careful on that river."

He knew where I was headed. It wasn't as if I'd come to do the weeding.

I had the key to the house but didn't bother using it. I thought about wandering down that broad, yawning hallway from antiquated décor close to the front door, to the stripped woods of the kitchen and the back door. Muddying up all that for just this short trip seemed wrong. So, I took the gravelled route past the stiff white walls, wall plants with bees that clung to me with a buzz I couldn't throw off my ears, and the scent of lilac, emanating from a still indistinct source. Red-hot pokers that still scared me a little and then down the mounds of sloping lawn to the tree-lined river. The raft.

I slipped onto the splintery planks and the whole plane bobbed. I sat down and took my secret out of the bottom of the bag – an old pen-knife, a gift from some random childhood boyfriend. Somehow, I'd never got around to throwing it out. I set to work, scraping the fibres of the rope holding the raft to the bank.

I knew when I started that it would take a while, but I had underestimated the strain on my hands. By the time I had finished, they ached from the effort and were sore with burns and indentations from the fibres. The raft did not move away quickly on release. You'd think after all those years, decades in fact, there would be a sense of sudden freedom, but it just kind of drifted. And when it drifted to a point where it would normally be reined back, it carried on drifting.

I lay down on my back, eyes closed to the sun. I felt something light upon my neck but left seconds before I brushed it away. Could have been a wasp, or just a dragonfly leaving its eggs, or a reed brushing past me.

I opened my eyes. There was a brown pony on the stubbled land on the other side of the water, and a kite rising with a jolt from the other side of the hill but the nearby sound of rushing water meant I couldn't hear the sounds of who was flying it.

I sat up and the raft rocked violently. My heart skipped a beat, even though I was safe, a strong swimmer. At worst, I would capsize myself and get wet, in which case, I would go into the house and stoke up the fire for the last time. I looked for Eleanor in my head. She was nothing to me, nothing but a lock to the door to what was left of my family. I'd locked it shut.

But more and more, I wanted to leave it alone.

So, what disturbed me about being so adrift? What can go wrong when you can swim? What can possibly be missing?

I had travelled a rather erratic path, a few yards down the river and glanced up to see my progress. I'd achieved what I came for, to be cut adrift, and was floating alone.

Now there was no Eleanor, Freddie and Dad, no Gemma and Robin. No husband or wife, son or father to lose. I really had cut loose. It was just a shock to lose them all so soon and so completely. I would get used to it. The sun was warm and the ripples gentle. I could be completely peaceful now.

III

Part Three

Chapter 12

Paternoster Sq - Copyright alexmorrall.com

Three of us staring at the film featuring Robin's mosaic (yeah, I still hang out with them), holding blue cardboard boxes of popcorn, conformists that we are. *From a black screen emerges a barely discernible light. By it, we can see an alleyway, a tangle of people – at least three. There is some sort of struggle going on. But it is too dark to understand what is really happening.*

In seconds, you know that someone has been hurt because he cries out, and then gasps for breath. The music is blurring the exact words being used. There are only men's voices. Then there is the sound of feet running away.

The dim light increases, slightly. The music has taken over on the audio. The light seems quite yellow, and you realise that its increase is due to the rising of the sun. Shadows spin out and shrink. Dawn is being sped up before your eyes. As soon as you realise this, you see what is on the floor.

There is a man on the floor. He is clearly the man who cried out. He is wearing the trousers of a suit, and a shirt. He is motionless in a cobbled street, and there is blood streaming from him. Large green doors to one side of him and many barred windows. The scene disappears.

The next scene is 'Sylvie' in a bathrobe with lank damp hair, opening a front door. She finds the police on her doorstep. They ask to come in and sit down. They tell her about the man on the cobbled street. They say he had an argument with the man in the club concealed by the green doors, and they tell Sylvie that the man is her husband.

But Sylvie does not believe them. Because she cannot imagine why her husband would be in such a place. He was a married man, they'd been talking about starting a family. He wasn't the type of person to be hanging out in fringe pubs and getting into fights.

And the police look at her sadly. They see nothing but double lives in this job, and here they have found another. Some guy with his young girlfriend, some guy who appears respectable with his wife he promises to have children with 'at some point'. Nothing too unusual.

The next time we see her. She is stirring a café latte in Zero Bar, a labyrinth of mirrors. She is with Ben and she is all questions, questions, questions. She has identified her husband's body, she tells Ben. But she cannot believe it. Did Ben have any idea of this double life? How can she have been so deceived? Does Ben know anything, anything at all that will help her disprove this whole affair? Surely, he must know something.

And Ben finally starts. He tells her that occasionally her husband, Peter, would get called by a man, oh, he can't think of the name right now, but he can find it at home, because at one point, Peter asked Ben to take a message for him.

Yes, Sylvie wants the name. She wants the name now. She will follow Ben home for it, right now.

Leave Ben alone Sylvie and move on, we think in the audience. It's just a name, the smallest shred of evidence.

I agreed to go to the film festival with Robin and Gemma because you can be hidden in the dark, and there is no need for conversation. I didn't fit in here. I think you need to go up and tell all the film people how wonderful they are and they will forgive you for being so minor an audience member as the friend of the man who made the backdrop of the film. Robin was thrilled. I didn't let myself wonder about his beating heart.

I made the right noises as people passed, nudging his arm and hissing congratulatory remarks. I didn't ask if his dad won the election and I didn't tell him the hard stuff, nothing emotional. I didn't tell him that I'd had a postcard from Montreal, the first news in a month since Dad and Eleanor had gone.

There are differences between my solitude and Sylvie's. Hers was forced upon her. Mine is a choice. I have made me.

Ben and the heroine agree to meet in Zero Bar with a quick phone call, where she calls, arranges the place, and then leaves Ben hovering – adrift on the dialling tone, without connection. He calmly places the receiver back onto the phone. The camera moves out of the phone booth, backwards. Through the reflections, we can see Ben lean down to pick up the sports bag at his feet and climb out onto the road. There is something about the turn of the camera that makes us think about Ben in a different light, that there might just be something we haven't understood about Ben up to now.

Zero Bar. The camera swings through the mirrors from the bar without apparently turning around. This re-introduction to a scene we know well is sinister. We know to be wary this time.

It must take agile camera work never to catch its own reflection and we find ourselves back where we started. Zero Bar. The bar of ultimate deceit, too confused by seeing what's behind you, or the vanity of seeing yourself to know where you're being taken.

Deceit. But we know exactly what's going on here.

Our heroine gets here first. She is dressed in ever-so-smart casual clothes, black pinstripe trousers, a smart sweater and a scarf. She's not trailing the seedy side of London now.

She hovers with her tea near the first eave of mirrors, so as to be visible to Ben when he arrives. She stirs the drink, casually runs her eyes over the reflection of her grey face, rings under her eyes. Our heroine is here to be deceived, we get surer of it. Now that our minds have been introduced to the possibility, we have run the net of our minds over previous scenes and gathered all the clues. Why hadn't we seen it before?

She stirs. Loud rock music starts generating waves as we swing through the mirrors, and as she sits there stirring, it eventually starts to fade away.

A lane of light fills the corner of the bar. Though we can't see it, we sense that a door has opened. Then the lane disappears. Ben stands near Sylvie.

Kisses on cheeks. Sylvie stands to get Ben's lager and to replace her tea with wine. She returns. They both sit. Ben reaches a hand to one of Sylvie's arms, both of which are laid across the table, reaching out to her glass of wine. "Sylvie, what is it?"

Don't tell him, Sylvie. Zero Bar is a place of deceit. But she looks down and sighs. "I'm nearly there."

"Nearly where, Sylvie?"

"I think I'm close to finding out what happened to Peter. I was following your lead."

"Well, tell me. Tell me what you've found."

A pause. She clicks her nails against the stem of her glass.

Ben pushes. "If you don't think you're ready." *He swallows.*

"I followed your lead."

"Yes." *Ben leans forward, gripped.*

"Followed them, oh, all over the place." *Yes. We saw the betting shops, the laundry chains, the strip joints. We learned how Sylvie got around without being caught out, such a nice girl for such a terrible place.* "I..." *Briefly, very briefly, tears flooded her throat. Then recovery.*

"I gave you a name," *jumps in Ben. Too impatient, he gives himself away so easily to our now wise ears.*

"Yes, you did." *The name of the man who Peter once mentioned, who must be involved in some plot, that spilled out sometimes, spilled out and burned Sylvie's husband.* "I got there, eventually. I got there. I found the man with the name." *She even spoke to him. We saw it.*

"I spoke to him."

Ben looks up oddly, paler than his usual pale. "You spoke to him?"

"Yes." The syllable is clear and loud and cool. "I grabbed him by the arm. I said, 'What have you done to my husband?'"

The audience is confused. That's not what happened. She bumped into him on the tube, spilled his coffee. She'd said, "Oh, I'm so sorry." He'd said, "Accidents happen." Then the sliding doors of the Circle Line separated them. No time for recriminations.

"You what?

"What do you think he said to me, Ben?"

He blushes again. "I... I couldn't say. He leans back in his chair as if to pull out of the collusion. The audience is getting up to speed again. This is Zero Bar, Sylvie's territory. We've seen her here so often. We should have guessed. Sylvie's grieving, she's not stupid. She's worked out Ben's tricks by now.

"He said..." But Sylvie doesn't have to continue. Ben's deceit had been flawless, effortless, and subtle, but now slightly tripped up, Ben cannot even begin to find ground. He shakes his head feebly. He looks like he needs permission to go to the toilet.

"If you lied about all of this, what lies did you tell Peter? What lies have you told me about Peter?" Her hand switches to his wrist, grabbing tightly. Ben pulls. His seat clatters beneath him, but his wrist is still held for a few seconds. They make eye contact. Ben and Sylvie's eyes meet, and then he pulls his wrist away, sharply, spilling the wine. He leaves his sports bag and runs out of the bar.

Vaguely, there is the sense that other customers, the bar staff, are looking, all eyes awake and shocked, their conversations stilled. But it is all in a blur because Sylvie is getting up and running after him. You can see it's an impulsive move, fury over sense because she's wearing heels. You're thinking, is this sensible? Ben may be pathetically built, but he's still a bloke, still taller than Sylvie and *likely stronger.*

When she has clambered up the steel steps and pushed her way out of the bar doors, she scans the street to find out where he has gone. Her cheeks are already red, her breath already laboured, but the moment she catches sight of him, just a few yards down the street, she runs again, furiously.

There is a market on the street, hanging slinky jeans and sexy T-shirts on white wire racks, suits with fluorescent posters declaring that they are all under fifty pounds, mosaics of different coloured sunglasses, heaps of hippy silver, boxes of shampoo and bootlegged media. She looks both ways, no sign. He could be behind any store or even at the end of the road.

A loud stallholder wants her to try on his shoes. They sit on their white cardboard box, inviting her to try them on. She ignores them and looks ahead. Swathes of curtain material, more shoddy cosmetics, busyness. He could be anywhere. Her pace stops and she steps out, out of the centre to the left-hand pavement.

And, because this is a film, there he is, all skinny and nervous and now running fast in the other direction, faster than Sylvie ever could. But she starts running again. Just as he turns off the street, he collides with two running teenagers, laughing as they go. He staggers and then Sylvie's arm is there, pushing him against the wall.

What must strike her now, is what on earth to do next as a woman in heels. But Ben is shivering, and not about to put up a fight. "Sylvie, I needed the money. I had to get that money. There are people after me. I owe them."

"And what are they going to do to you when they find you?" she demanded. There's a silence. We see the camera pull slightly away from them. The alley off the market street is dark, grey and cobbled. There is the occasional barred window and large green bolted door. And we realise. Sylvie starts looking around. She seems to realise

with us. This is the alley where her husband's body was found. The green doors are the exit of the club he'd allegedly gone inside and rowed with his murderer.

"What are they going to do when they find you, Ben? Are they going to stab you in a place like this? What on earth would make you think that they're that dangerous?"

Ben starts to choke. His knees buckle and Sylvie loosens her grip on him. Ben is crying dry tears, struggling for breath. "It wasn't my fault," *he wails. He has reached his knees, his jeans in the dust. Sylvie pulls away, rubbing her hands against her coat as if trying to rub him off.*

"How..." *Now Sylvie is losing her words to hoarseness.* "... can it not be...?"

"I saw one of them. In the club. It was only half ten. All I could think to do was call Peter to protect me. Two better than one, you know." *More choking.* "When he arrived, did he look out of place in the smoke, dressed in half a suit like he'd just popped in after work? I guess that's what caught people's attention. That's why they saw me when I neared him. I knew that it was time to run and I pulled Peter with me. He was acting stupid, like 'Ben what's the problem? I just paid to get in.' But he saw sense in following me, rather than just hanging about.

We got to the doors and fell into the alley. And it was pitch black. That light," he points to a streetlamp above them, *"it wasn't on. So as soon as me and Peter, as soon as those guys were out and the door closed, you couldn't see a thing. I was still running. I assumed Peter was behind me. But he must have stopped, tried to work out where his feet were in the black, or something. He couldn't have known what was at stake."*

Sylvie has calmed down. Her breath is caught back and her arms limp at her sides. "So, they got Peter, assuming he was you. Is that *what you're saying?"*

"I think so."

"And you didn't go back?" Anger rises towards the end of the question. "You didn't go back?"

"What could I have done?"

Sylvie's palms scrabble back at Ben's face, angry as birds, useless as butterflies. "Coward! You coward. You coward." Ben's hands push away hers, holding her by the wrists.

"I'm sorry. I'm sorry." He cries harder.

Sylvie pulls away again, watches the pathetic heap. Again: what to do now? Her handbag has slipped to the floor, her hair is all about her face. She rearranges herself and picks up her bag. We start to see that she is also crying. She lifts her chin slightly into the air. "I'm calling the police," she says. He seems to cry harder. She starts walking away, her heels clicking onto the cobbles. She lets a small contemptuous breath release from her mouth.

But as she walks away from the drama, she walks beneath Robin's mosaic, its bottle-top hills, and chugging lardas, the eucalyptus trees on the horizon, and the lining of the yellow sky with bright white, and we realise, that Robin's mosaic means hope.

"Are you alright?" asked Gemma, peering with concern into my white face, as we came into daylight. She treated me the way she wished I would treat her. "You don't look well. Robin said you'd been a bit quiet lately." Robin had wandered off into the love-in with the producer and the scriptwriter.

I blinked at Gemma. She seemed to be a million miles away from me and it was all my own fault. The film had ended with rock music and it was screaming through my head. Behind us, a tinny voice was repeating the first line of a joke – a question that the listener could not catch. Someone spoke over the punchline but I could tell from the listener's "Oh, I get it," that she hadn't heard the start.

"Are you coming to the party?"

I shrugged. The film had made my head spin, unnerved me. I looked to one side of Gemma, not meeting her eye. "Can't. Got to get back to work. Story to unravel."

Chapter 13

There was no specific story to unravel. I just needed to escape. The office was empty and cold. The lights came on as I swiped my pass through the barriers. I gathered a pile of mail from the floor to sort into the pigeonholes, a newbie job I hadn't managed to pass on to anyone else yet. A few of the large Manila envelopes were addressed to me. I flicked through, waiting for something to catch my eye, and saw Mr Tadesse's looping handwriting. I held the envelope separate from the others, the man continuing to hope for justice despite my inability to help. I brought it over to the kitchenette to open as I kicked off the vending machine.

The machine's instant coffee generation seemed unusually loud in the empty office as I ripped the seal open to find several documents. I laid the glossy leaflets and folded plans out on the countertop, knowing that I should not get involved. I should return it all unread and be honest with Mr Tadesse about my limitations. But not to open it felt like missing an opportunity to honour Mr Tadesse's son. I pulled at the A4 handwritten letter accompanying it, and more papers flicked out onto the floor. As I stopped to gather them, the sponsorship logos of one glossy charity document caught my eye, the chairman's name underneath and a photocopy of a cheque for a phenomenal amount of money, and the name Hawk.

'Mr Hawk' fell onto the floor, looking like the prime suspect of the scandal thousands of miles away. At first, I smiled at the name of my friend, noticing and then dismissing as I always do, something that reminded me of Robin Hawk.

But then I could see how strange a coincidence it was to link that name to a country that Robin had visited.

There is something about the turn of the camera that makes us think about Ben in a different light, that there might just be something we haven't understood about Ben up to now.

I thought of ringing Robin to tell him my discovery. In the middle of the film festival. That would be welcome. So I was left pondering the letter alone.

When I tell stories of Robin Hawk's life and I include the details about what he ate and how the weather was, not exactly truths, but good enough to make Robin real, I keep all the major parts of the story in place. Haven't we talked philosophy and politics and girlfriends, and the film world enough to know that he is not corrupt or evil? Knowing those things without ever having discussed them. "By the way, Robin, on a scale of one to ten, how much would you be prepared to put lives at risk through shoddy work, or saving money if no one who knew you, knew about the lives? Just curious." But why would he? He'd never seemed to care about money. At least, not until he knew he'd needed to escape the dusty intellectual world that would have given him a basic job.

At home, I stared at my reflection in the mirror. Once the thought had registered, encouraged by the moody distrustful tone of the film, I'd hardly had the heart to stay and relax with them. What was I going to do with the evening now? Probably sit in front of the TV trying to conjure up reasons and excuses for Robin, against the backdrop of garish game shows and ads for even cheaper insurance, forgetting who I was and what Ethiopia, or Robin, had to do with anything anymore.

I should ask him.

And he would say, "What are you talking about, Bernie? There are thousands of people with Hawk as a last name in the world. Is my name on your mind too much?"

Like Sylvie, working out Ben's game, I saw Robin had needed the money. So, he sets up a partnership to fulfil a needed job, perhaps with a good heart, but sees a way of keeping a bit of money back himself. And it's tempting because he is on the verge of being part of a fantastic creative project that might not happen if he can't find the money. And Robin, as you know, is a risk taker.

But I just didn't believe that this was something that Robin could have done.

Cowardice won. I went to the computer to email him but ended up messaging him when I found him online. It surprised him, I think, that I flew to the facts the moment his sudden "hello, there," flashed onto the screen.

"I've stumbled on something," I began. "I wondered if you'd seen anything of it when you were in Ethiopia." I told him the story, leaving out that I knew the name involved.

There was no return message for a while. I sipped at my rapidly cooling coffee. I checked my bank balance for a few seconds, then it came through.

"That's terrible. But why are you telling me?"

My turn to return to silence for a while. I thought about writing, "I just wondered…" Better than, "I just suspected…"

"Thought you would be curious. Coincidences. You having been to the country." I waited a few moments before adding, "I saw something with the name 'Hawk' on it." And I knew I could trust him to know that this was no veiled attack or interrogation. I only needed the facts to be reassured of my confidence in Robin.

I asked myself how I could know, but I knew the answer already. I knew Robin. Robin and I trusted each other.

And his connection went dead.

Chapter 14

No matter what you are, how happy, beautiful, social, or clever, you won't be able to fly. This must sometimes occur to Robin, especially if you think how fast he can walk with those long, long legs. He will walk like that along crowded streets, with his mind soaring in unreal worlds. He must think that he is flying. And then he has to wait behind ten tourists at a pelican crossing. Or perhaps he will be running late and be reminded that his route from Charing Cross to Covent Garden would be much quicker as the crow flies.

Oh, I know. I'm not supposed to be here with him, or believing that I am with him, knowing how he thinks.

Ideas. Ideas are what Robin's got, like a flock of pigeons lifting, soaring and colliding within the confines of his mind. Your head's only got so much space in it. Which must be good news for some people, I suppose. Just not for Robin.

They've a rhythm, those birds – but you know, how does Robin know it's not someone else's rhythm fluttering up on him? The pigeons wouldn't be able to tell him that they're not his ideas.

He wasn't in the West End right then, a couple of hours after we spoke on the web. The weather had dried out to a sudden crispness. The cinemas and theatres of Soho were so accomplished, so exposed to audiences that the magic had sanded down of all of its coarseness, its independence that they were like shiny marbles to be split amongst 'the consumer', and he'd started walking in the other direction.

Robin's mood was more confused than fits a polished world. He'd come across a market. It was a Saturday, a packed market, of every fruit imaginable. Piles of fruit reminded him of his teaching days in Ethiopia. Ginger roots like beautiful minds of sweet mysterious spice within the brown withered exterior; passion fruit open with the blood-red interiors. Robin looked at the sweet things but he could only smell the salt, the grey of a nearby fish store.

Robin was a magician and the people around him didn't seem to have noticed. Robin saw a good deal on a set of mugs. He saw two impossibly young teenage girls painted with jewellery and cigarettes, trying on impossibly high shoes.

This was where Robin needed to fly because even as he tried

to walk behind the stalls, he found more crowds. Robin had his hands in his pockets but he still wanted to walk faster. Even though he didn't know where he was going. He was just trying to walk out the nagging thought of Hawk and Ethiopia.

The pavement was grey and ruptured beneath the poles supporting the canvas canopies, bunching at the base and litter clustered about their feet. It had started to rain. It felt like the grey sky knew it was no different from the ground and let itself fall. Robin felt a slight irritation. But nothing changed. His phone was ringing. Gemma?

Over the yells of "Stacey, you got change for a fiver?" Robin could hear Mike, an old school friend asking if he wanted to meet for a few drinks later, or perhaps now, even. He was back in the West End. Did Robin know anywhere worth visiting?

Zero Bar was aptly named for achieving oblivion, Robin had often joked, although until now he had never personally taken advantage of the name. Mike repeated the joke back at him when he had suggested meeting there and Robin said, "Oh, yeah. I never thought of that," because the market had started to loudly dismantle about him and explanations were not worth the time. "It'll be a great nostalgia trip."

Robin had the feeling he was supposed to be seeing Gemma that evening. He called to check as he lifted himself from the dusty market via the gum-lined steps to the station. In this case, I happened to know. Gemma's work friend, Ashley, was holding a housewarming party and Gemma and Robin were invited. She had told Robin a while back. When she reminded him, he remembered. "I'm going for a couple of drinks with an old friend first," he told her. "I'll catch you there. He's so cool. He's trying to become a performance poet."

The creative days roared back to life as he pushed through the bar doors, the strain of negotiating funding, keeping true to his vision but staying relevant to the funding demands, difficulties now sunk into the lighter memories of sculpting the mosaic. He took a stool at the bar and let Mike wander in amongst the mirrors to discover the maze that they made himself. He wasn't in the mood to repeat the experience.

Years ago, when practising the art of alcohol at university, Robin had drunk, unmixed, unrocked whiskeys, advocaat, white rum – a rainbow of rums – vodka, fortified wines and, well, everything.

Now he saw these precious stones of bottles studded behind this bar and everyone around him was drinking wine, not out of stemmed glasses, but still with the 250ml mark embossed centimetres from the top.

A couple of drinks ago. He would have reminded himself that he was now a grown up with a real job and a real girlfriend, but there was something about the old-fashioned label on the small bottle, the myths of poets on creative trips and the comparison of liquor, of wormwood, with ideas that thump like pigeons which made absinthe seem to fit his jaded state of mind. It would make Robin think that he was flying.

"Equivalent of seven pints, isn't it?" asked Mike with boyish glee as the bartender fulfilled the order.

Robin thought it was an exaggerated pretence but didn't want to disappoint Mike. "At least," he said. So, Robin chose to embrace the night, entering darkness.

And while I was trying not to think about Robin, I glanced at the clock and noticed it turn half-past nine, about the time I imagine Robin staggered out of Zero and reached Gemma's party. It's impossible to describe how, with his head flying in the desired oblivion, his body with the cohesion of an amoeba, the details of his journey only known by him as they occurred, and possibly not even then. But what was remembered, was seeing her, in someone else's front room, looking at him crossly, and it is a moment where Robin briefly retrieved the clarity of mind to wonder why Gemma was cross with him.

He started leaning backwards but collapsed against the dark wood shelving his hand had reached out for. A perfect blue vase fell with him and split, just the one break at the neck, on the carpet. Two pieces. He lay there for a few moments like a broken puppet. Didn't you feel pity there, Gemma? Just for a few seconds, pity? The broken vase, the broken face of someone defeated. Even if he was about to throw it in your face, you must have felt pity. Even though you'd no idea about the texts that I'd sent which hurt him so much.

He had flailed out to steady himself as if he had not yet fallen. I imagine he saw you. You had your hands on your hips. A bare light bulb hung beyond your head, dazzling him, casting you as some sort of interrogator. And those dark shadows of paranoia in Robin's head were there. They only needed to be woken up by an alcoholic episode.

Much of the party continued, oblivious to him. There were dancers out there with their eyes closed, their personal low-key alcoholic oblivion. But Robin would not have seen them. He would only have seen the shadows of the people centred on him. He brought an arm across his face to defend himself from that light. "How much have you had to drink?" demanded Gemma, which for Gemma, I would say, was weak.

Robin was vaguely aware that his sense of humour and charm normally solved awkward situations. Unfortunately, he was not aware of the complete details of the situation, other than that it was awkward. He forgot he was not capable of a good joke. "I've been on orange juice all evening."

Gemma snorted.

Robin could probably tell he was not going in the right direction but must have believed that it might get funnier if he continued. "I was out with an old school friend who believes only in the consumption of citrus fruit. So, I drank orange to fit in and he drank very pure lemonade."

"You met up with Mike. You told me." Gemma explained to herself. I expect she wondered what to do now. Could she try and pull him off the floor? But he was so huge and she was so small.

Ashley, tall, elegant Ashley, was standing beside her, holding a cocktail glass in her beautifully manicured hands and seemed to take in the situation mathematically. "Is there anything I can do to help, Gemma?" It was a gesture of support, but Gemma felt ashamed that Ashley's vase was broken and Robin was collapsed on Ashley's floor.

"I'd better call a taxi," she said quietly.

"No, no, no, no, no..." Robin held onto the last 'no' to the point where it must have ceased to be comical even to him. "We're all having such fun." Even though they both knew he was incapable of sarcasm, it was so far from the truth it was an insult.

Gemma tutted. "May I borrow your phone?"

"Of course. It's in the hallway."

Gemma, her arms crossed, turned her back on Robin. "Ashley, I am so sorry about this," she began.

"Don't leave me, Gemma," Robin called out to her back in response to the chill of her gesture. "I didn't mean any harm." As Gemma walked to the hallway, she heard Robin start to cry.

"The taxi journey was the worst thing in the world," Gemma said in between a flurry of jazz notes. We'd met for cappuccinos in Jazz, the following Sunday afternoon. Gemma had lowered her voice as I ordered them from the guy in white behind the bar. He threw them across the bar, eyes half-closed against the shrieking of the coffee machine, and the sax, bada, bada, baa….

She carried her cake, a refined type with powdered icing sugar that it would not have occurred me to buy, to a table where I put the coffees down. I pulled up a chair beside her. "I couldn't have made conversation if I'd wanted. And he stank. It was all I could do to convince the driver to take us. He was sure that Robin would throw up in the cab."

"He didn't?"

Gemma was using a plastic fork, putting it down at polite intervals as she told me the story. "Fortunately, after we got out. Straight after, outside his own house. The driver was waiting for me. I basically pushed him through the front door and left him there. By the time I'd succeeded in getting his keys off him, I felt I'd done enough."

"I get that."

She paused, folding the wrapping of her cake. "You know, he kept talking about his dad."

"His dad?"

"Yes, but you know, as if his dad was the one who was messing up, as if he was the one who was staggering around, throwing up, making a scene at a party."

I frowned at my drink. Oh. Robin's dad.

Chapter 15

I drove home in the dark, piecing the story together – Robin's complete lack of recognition about the story when I texted him, but the fact that it had disturbed him enough to end up over-drinking. The discovery I had made had never been about Robin. It was his hated father, whose attention might have turned to Ethiopia for his education charity for no other reason than his son had spent time there.

Was it my isolation that allowed the distrust in me? What do we ever know about anyone anyway? Are all of our connections only about emotion? How can you trust emotion? Maybe Gemma now feels misled by emotion, as I have been misled by facts. And when I think of emotion, I think of the river of my feelings for Robin again, failed and unacknowledged. I neared a slow white lorry, lit by the orange road lamps and indicated to overtake. No one was behind me. I began to move into the second lane, only to see a motorcycle coming in my direction. What was I doing? I was sure this had been a dual carriageway.

And the lorry blared and braked. And the bike did the same, the expression of its shocked driver obscured by his helmet. He swerved as I reached a gap to pull into, swerved around me, nearly missing me? I had no idea. My head was full of the lights and the horn and the panic.

Shaking, I pulled off the road as soon as possible and stopped in a shabby anonymous residential road. I was attacked by worry in all directions. Another second, another few seconds, how far from killing the biker, or myself? Robin and Jonathon Hawk. Fathers and sons. How deep was what I had revealed?

My mobile was in my glove compartment. I was high in adrenaline. He didn't answer his home phone. I tried again in case my cold white fingers had misdialled but it still rang and rang and rang.

So, I tried the mobile. It had been a long time since that familiar, fond string of numbers had appeared on my phone. I had got into the habit of calling Gemma when I wanted to speak to either of them.

"...llo," it answered. I always wondered if he swallowed the first syllable or had started the greeting before getting the handset to his mouth.

And the adrenaline rush dissipated. I couldn't say, Robin, I've just reported your dad to the Charity's Commission, or I've nearly been in a driving accident. I tried breathing,

"Bernie?"

I was in a shabby car on a dark corner in South London. I hadn't even turned on the inside light in the car. It was cold. Shadows of occasional people passed on the sidewalk, moving with drugged lunacy.

"Are you okay?"

"A motorbike came straight for me," I began. As I said it, it sounded ridiculous to attribute the bike with the attack. On the whole, I don't think I'd be the loser.

"Are you hurt?"

"No." I wanted to cry in response to Robin's concern about something that hadn't happened, as if I had somehow defrauded him. I resisted it. "I missed it, but now..." But now I couldn't find the willpower to start up the engine again. I didn't know how to word it.

"Where are you?"

"Croydon."

"Where exactly?"

I detailed the precise location in a small high-pitched voice, not daring to hope that he was offering to help me. "It's my fault. I wasn't concentrating." In case he should come all that way and discover that it was all my fault and go home again.

"I'm coming. Don't worry about it, Bernie." The phone went dead. He hadn't told me where he was coming from, or how he would find me.

I thought about starting the car up and driving away, pretending that this had never happened, leaving the space for Robin to wonder if he had dreamt the whole episode. But I couldn't have found the energy, even if I'd dared.

My toes got colder. My nose got colder. I hunched over in front of the steering wheel. I watched the headlights rise in the back window and diminish into red lights ahead of me. Each one gave me a chance to look at my watch. It had been a quarter of an hour since the call. I didn't know how Robin was going to reach me. I didn't know if I had dreamt the call.

I didn't mind the passing cars. It was the passing pedestrians that worried me. Not the couples, but the tall leaning figures, hands in pockets, faceless as they looked down. Walkers who had a better chance of working out that my car was occupied by a lone female. The far door was locked but the one near me wasn't. I was huddled by now in a scarf and my collar pulled up to my ears when the first stranger passed. I thought if I moved, they would see me. I sat, hearing myself breathe so loudly until eventually, I couldn't hear his footsteps anymore. I slipped a hand out and clicked down the lock.

Another car passed, another twenty minutes. What had happened to me? I was supposed to be the independent graduate who lived alone. And now I was shivering in a car, trying to pretend I didn't exist.

The next set of headlights came right to the boot of my car and stopped, glaring into my hiding place. My pulse raced. A door opened and he got out. Robin's silhouette in the cold night. He was leaning into the driver's window and talking to someone. I was trying to work out why he had a car until it drove away and I realised it was a taxi.

He pulled at the handle of the passenger seat with a dull click until I unlocked it. He sat down next to me. "I'm sure I owed you a taxi ride from sometime years ago," he said.

I looked out at him from within my cocoon.

"What's happened, Bernie?" He put a hand on my arm. I

113

shivered again. The image of the lorry and bike swerving came again, sickening.

But I said. "Hawk was your dad."

He laughed quietly and stared out of my windscreen. "Funny that."

"No, no. I mean, he's the one with the school and..." so cold and confused, I thought I had to explain, and then stopped.

"The thought had crossed my mind. Killed the details with a bit of an alcoholic episode, though."

"I've referred it to the Charity's Commission – I had to."

"It's okay, you know."

"The theory goes that he appropriated funds from the charity when times were hard; probably put them on the stock market intending to return the original amount and then lost it. Then had to botch the building work with no money." I paused. "The Charity's Commission mentioned the police."

Robin nodded. "Concise legalistic overview." He didn't look angry. He pursed his lips. "Some kid died there, yeah?"

"Yeah. My contact... it was his son." There was a silence. "We've passed the details to the police," I repeated.

Robin exhaled and looked at me. "I'm sure this isn't the only instance. Just the most unfortunate." He studied my face. "It doesn't matter to me the way you think it does, Bernie."

I closed my eyes. I felt warmer. I wanted to say, I didn't think that it would, but I couldn't summon the conviction.

"I thought I was here because you nearly drove into a motorbike."

I nodded, but I couldn't laugh, yet.

"Bernie," he began. Then quicker, "Bernie, you can cry."

But I shouldn't. And wouldn't. Instead, I caved into him. His arm was already reaching over to my shoulder and I hung, my muscles aching over the gap between the chairs. I tried to remember if we had hugged like this before. I supposed it was safe now that Gemma was in his life.

After a while, he lifted me up and looked at my face. I think he was looking for tears, smudged mascara, but he said nothing when he saw nothing. "Shall I drive us back?"

"It's alright. I think I can do it. I just needed there to be someone else in the car."

"We haven't had a good talk for ages you and I," he said as we drove towards Gemma's.

"I've been so busy...."

"I suppose so. Hey, me and Gem are meeting some friends at the pub tomorrow night. You should join us."

After the intimacy of his brief conversation about his dad, the evening's label was being written. Bernie and Robin were platonic friends who got to chat occasionally.

Friday night down by the river is where all the people from my drained-out city had apparently gone. All of them. Packed into a few small pubs, they drank amber liquid and cast amber light onto the banks with their newly amber souls.

"We're never going to find them." I had pulled the sleeves of my coat over my hands and pulled the collar up. I was looking at the second vacuum-packed bar we had passed. People were even out leaning on the icy benches of the beer gardens, others had their legs hanging over either side of the walls of the banks with more empty glasses than full, staring at black water. Laughter seemed to be everywhere.

"We will, just be patient."

I glanced at Gemma. She looked about as convinced as I was. She'd given me a bit of a 'glad you're here' smile as I'd joined them, still aware of what had happened last time she'd been out with Robin.

"You'd only survive for a few seconds in that water, on a day like this," Robin ambled on. I looked up. It was starting to cloud over. Grey clouds were obscuring the legs and belt of Orion. The rest was shrouded in a thin pink cloud.

Robin stopped and turned around. He was wearing that, 'my phone is vibrating' look. Confirming this, he pulled it out of his pocket and answered.

"We've just walked past them," he explained, putting the phone away. "They were outside the first pub." As we walked back, hoots of raucous laughter rose from the walls. Three guys stood there, looking at us, looking at Robin.

"Hey there." It seemed Robin knew only one of them, shaking hands with the other two, and exchanging names. Then Gemma and I were introduced to Mark, a skinny guy with curls and curls of dark hair; Steve, slightly shorter and chubbier; and Ted. Ted was Robin's contact. He had gel-ruffled sandy hair. He also had a red face and a slimy mouth – too many pints of lager.

"What are you drinking?"

Gemma and I ordered glasses of wine. Robin, a pint of lager.

"You're driving, Robin," Gemma prodded him, prompting glances from all three strangers.

"Make it a coke," he said, without looking at Gemma. I saw her turn slightly, the reaction from not being acknowledged. I noticed Steve had seen, too. Robin went to help with the drinks.

Steve moved towards Gemma and slipped an arm around her waist. "So, what do you do for a living," he slurred.

"I work for an art's PR agency." Her body was spikey, trying

116

not to object to the arm, but at the same time minimise the contact with Steve.

"I'm a musician. Do you do PR for musicians?"

Gemma shook her head.

"Musicians not good enough, hey? Turning me down before I've even shown you my work."

Gemma smiled a lost-at-sea smile. "Have you seen my boyfriend's work?"

"Whaddoes he do?"

"He's a mosaicist."

"Oh, that will be how Ted knows him," Steve mumbled, as Ted and Robin returned with the drinks. Robin took a sidelong, but unintrusive glance at Steve's arm around Gemma and then continued to talk to Ted. Fragments of conversation drifted my way. It sounded like they were discussing a film from the festival that they liked by a guy they hated. Gemma continued her awkward conversation and I felt like I was falling into another world outside of both conversations. By now, I was sitting on the stone wall and as frozen as the stone itself.

"Whose round is it?" came a bellow from Steve to no reply. "I've had an empty glass for ages now. Whose round is it?"

"I think that it's yours," began Ted.

"I've bought thousands of drinks," said Steve looking vacantly at the empty glass in the hand not around Gemma, with an expression of knowing he was wrong, but not prepared to admit it.

"It's definitely yours," said Mark.

Steve looked up, his lower jaw pushed out. "It is not mine." The words were strung out slowly.

"I'll get a round," volunteered Robin.

"You got the last one," hissed Steve. He had now released

Gemma from his arm, but she seemed too polite to move completely away.

"I think Robin was just..." tried Ted.

Steve jumped in. "I know what Robin was just doing, he was, he was..." Everyone, everyone could see the tension winding up in Steve, his shoulders arching and voice raising. Now it started cascading out as he struggled for the words, but instead of finding the words he launched into Ted.

Now Gemma stepped away as the blokes, Robin included, stepped in. There were raised indistinguishable words of, "Hey, Steve," and "Let's all just calm down," as the four of them merged into a machine unit centred about Steve.

Just as they seemed to achieve equilibrium, Steve exploded again, landing a fist on Robin. Again, all hands were on Steve, but Robin was ruining the balance now, his voice raised too loud, too loud for the evening river. And his hands were reaching out to Steve before he was pulled back. Steve was being pulled back too, too far, as his foot behind him struggled with the step and crashed into the water, shortly followed by the rest of his body.

Two seconds of silence before the splashing reached our ears.

Gemma, Gemma was white.

Pulling the spluttering feet like a game of tug of war and the group separated into two across the muddy grass, split by the mist of their breath in the cold air. "Come on, Steve. We were just having a night out," breathed Ted. The air tightened and then became reluctant.

Steve shook himself.

"I'm going home," he mumbled and picked up a bag from the wall, dripping as he went, and trying to act as if he wasn't. He swung it onto his back and marched off towards the bridge.

Robin seemed to relax as he got out of earshot, but not entirely. The height of the magician's body made it easier to tangle. "We all still have empty glasses," he tried.

Mark laughed. He slapped Robin's shoulder. "I guess that makes it my round now." He joined the crowds of the beer garden.

"You mean we're staying?" breathed Gemma, faintly.

Robin glanced at her, at first surprised and then expressionless. "Yeah, it's cool. Steve's gone. Right?"

Gemma shrugged, her lips pressed tightly together. The spritzer she had ordered was still only half drunk. I caught Ted's eye. He looked a little scared of Gemma, as scared as you can get when you're that drunk. Robin, however, was choosing not to notice.

By the time the drinks came out, we had divided into clear boy-girl lines. Gemma talking to me about her boss, or something. It was clear her mind wasn't on the subject. I could hear catches of Robin's conversation. "Yeah, I didn't think much of that scene either." His voice was also lacking in concentration, trying to relax.

"You want to go home?" I eventually risked asking Gemma.

She closed her eyes in resignation and nodded faintly. "He's driving," she reminded me, glancing in Robin's direction without looking at him.

"We could go back on the tube. Just leave him having a night with the boys."

Gemma tried to smile. Perhaps she was worried that it would look as if she were storming off. She could try and explain it, but she didn't look as if she were in the state to do anything so composed. Robin looked over, though, and broke the siege.

"Did you want to get back?"

Gemma said nothing.

"I think that we were only planning to come for a quick pint," I called instead.

"Yeah, I know." As if to make the decision easier, large drops of rain started falling, making ripples in the river. Robin finally looked relaxed. "Well, good to see you again, Ted," he said. "Nice night," he tried after a couple of yards. "Just a pity about the preliminary episode," he added when neither of us said anything.

"You didn't know him, right?" I asked.

"No, they were just mates of Ted's, from work, or something. It was good to see Ted again, though."

I nodded. I couldn't think of anything to say to this. Then Gemma spoke. "Maybe you could meet your friends in your own time next time," she said softly.

Robin looked confused and then angered. "Pardon?"

"That's not how I meant it," she answered.

Robin looked over at Gemma quizzically.

"I mean that I am furious with you for dragging us out on your lad's night, ignoring me when I'm getting too much attention from one of them, and then getting involved in a, a ... pub brawl."

"You didn't look like you were exactly fighting off Steve's attentions," Robin muttered.

"No, that's right, I enjoy plastered idiots draping themselves over me."

Silence. We had reached the end of the riverside pathway and started to climb the steps to the bridge. I wondered how we were going to get there without Robin exploding.

"I just wanted to meet a friend I had met at the film festival. I didn't know he'd have such great company or had had so much to drink."

Gemma shrugged. We had reached the car. I started looking in my pockets for my keys, forgetting that Robin had them. He was already starting to open the car. I was cold, waiting for him to open the passenger door, and tired. I slipped into the back. Gemma followed in the front. "You could have kept Steve away from me, though," Gemma suddenly added.

There was a tut and a clearing of the throat as Robin started up the engine. Please leave it at that Robin. The length, the density of my day was beginning to take its effect on me. I was closing my eyes and the petrol smell was floating. I was floating, somewhere else. I could hear voices a long way away, and then abruptly, the door clicked open.

I thought, *oh, shut the door, Gemma. It's too cold and wet.* Then I noticed that she was stepping out, at first with her seatbelt still on, then she clicked it apart and wound it back, stepping into the rain. Her coat was still on the back seat next to me and she stood clutching her folded arms to herself, hunching her shoulders in just her silver shirt to protect her from the rain. Robin shot out moments afterwards, as I thought, *don't do that Robin, now we will never get home.* They had both tried to slam their doors behind them, but on Gemma's side, the tilt of the road meant that it swung halfway shut and then flew open again. And I was too cold, too confused by their new row.

"What did you think you were doing? Don't you care? I don't get you. Don't you care?"

I was straining to hear the words, hear Gemma throwing out bitterness. I was torn between analysing the new phenomena and wishing myself out of the situation. I sat with my knees against the back seat and my head bent over them, trying to

121

hide, pretend I wasn't there. I wondered if there was a book, or a mini-disc in my bag to take my mind off the situation.

The orange streetlights highlighted the damp locks of Gemma's hair and Robin's angry face, on the verge of losing his temper.

It was only when Robin came back in, landing in the driver's seat and slamming the door behind him, that it struck me what had happened. He stared at his lap for a few moments. I couldn't see his face, just the downwards sloping curve of his neck. I wondered why I could still hear the rain and realised that Gemma's door was still wide open. "She's gone," he said, his tone completely empty. I had been selfishly wishing the argument over. They had been splitting up.

"Gone where?" I looked hopelessly at the spot where she had disappeared around the corner as if she would rematerialise.

"Well, I don't know, do I?" The first half of the sentence was shouted, the second strained. "I'm sorry," he added hoarsely.

The passenger door was still gaping. I glanced over and thought about shutting it, to apologise for my stupid question. But I would have had to move into Gemma's seat in the front. I didn't feel able to take her place. Even though it was odd, me in the back and him in the front. He didn't ask me to move either. We sat watching the rain running over the interior, tapping where it hit the floor. My car was being spoiled and I didn't really care. Finally, Robin reached over towards the passenger door and shut it. I should have become capable Bernie, taken over, looked after Robin and made him happier. But I didn't know where Gemma had gone either. I didn't know the words. "I'm sorry," seemed the only thing I could say.

He was drenched, everywhere dripping. At the same time as desperately shivering out of sympathy for him, I remembered that Gemma's coat was still there beside me. As I was thinking it, he caught my eyes in the front mirror, so I didn't have to worry about whether to mention it or not. He knew what I had realised.

"We could drive around and see if we find her."

He straightened his shoulders. "You don't really think that she wants to be found, do you?"

I felt around near the coat and in its pockets. "I think she has her purse."

He drew his eyes from mine and nodded. "I think I saw her with it."

"The station isn't so far away."

"Look, Bernie, if you think we should go after her, it's up to you."

Thanks, Robin. Put the burden on me. "Do you want to?"

He turned around in his seat and looked at me. "Bernie, she's just walked out on me."

I nodded. "Okay."

Robin turned back and switched on the ignition. A road of falling raindrops ahead of us was highlighted. He still hadn't suggested that I move into the front seat. I think then I knew he knew that there was some big deal between us. And he'd assumed that I'd cottoned on ages ago.

To be honest, I hoped as we drove the roads back towards London, that we wouldn't see Gemma on the road that night. The chapter was written. I was dead tired and Robin didn't want me in the car with him.

Chapter 16

I didn't hear from either of them for a while. I guessed they needed their space and I tried to find new stories hidden amongst the leads work left me. I went in one day to find a man standing by my desk, tall, slim and black in a linen suit that seemed just slightly too large. It was rare for me to have any visitors here. The sort of clients I dealt with were usually just telephone conversations.

He was reaching to shake my hand while I was still on the other side of the gap between desks. "You know, when you first contacted me about the inheritance from my wife's family,

I just assumed you were scammers," he told me in a quiet but very authoritative tone.

"Mr Tadesse?"

He nodded. "I wanted to come by personally and say thank you. We have been devastated by this sadness." Although his voice sounded surprisingly neutral, I could believe in the cloud that darkened his heart. I knew about the cloud so well. For most of my life, my dad had lived through one.

"Your recommendations have been invaluable. There is a case being made by the CPS now."

My recommendation had been nothing more than to refer the case to the Charity's Commission. Mr Tadesse had done all the research that provided the basis for the evidence more professionally than if he was in my role, but I didn't want to not acknowledge the thanks. I stumbled on the words, "I hardly did anything..."

He smiled reassuringly at my awkwardness. "It appears Mr Hawk gathered charity funds, dipped in for his own needs, and then was unable to deliver on his public charity commitments without resorting to corner-cutting in health and safety." I winced, hopefully only to myself at the mention of the name 'Hawk' and all that had meant for my friends. "Your considerate replies to my letters were also appreciated."

I was relaxed by his persistent gentleness. "Can I offer you a vending machine coffee?" I waved my hand at the two shabby plastic chairs by the humming coke machines at the end of the office.

"That would be lovely," he said, as if I had offered him champagne. He joined me on the seats.

"What will you do now?"

"I'll be going back to start again, my volunteer work, and

maybe even start a new family."

"Really?" I knew that I sounded shocked and immediately collapsed into shyness. After everything, he wanted to start again? I was horrified, but I couldn't enunciate it. It was none of my business, and my shocked comment hung in the air along with the tang of instant coffee granules.

He watched me, and it surprised me to see the corners of his eyes smiling despite the sadness within them. I was struggling to work out whether he understood that I had my own stories of loss, or whether he was so well brought up to automatically put anyone he was talking to at ease. "There is only to keep on living, to keep the happiness of new things alongside the sorrow of lost things."

I stared at the floor. His words didn't resonate with me. One of my colleagues broke the silence passing by. "Bernie, is this a client? There's beer for clients in the fridge in the boardroom."

The message light on my mobile was flashing wildly when Mr Tadesse eventually left us. I was cold, but warm with beer. I listened to the network's scratchy voice at the other end tell me how many messages I had and what number to press to get rid of them. The first was about work. The second: a fractional breath, like a glimpse of a sigh, then cut off. The third: "Bernie, it's Robin. Please call me back."

I looked down at my desk, now with four empty *Peroni* bottles lying on it, the signs of new friendships and sadness. It was a week since the row between Robin and Gemma. This was the first I had heard from either of them.

"Robin."

"Bernie?"

"You called me?"

126

"Yeah, yeah." The voice was distant and distracted. "She's gone. Did you know?"

"Gone?"

"Away. On holiday, or perhaps for good. You didn't know then?"

I shook my head down the phone. Surely Gemma would not leave without telling me. Weren't we still friends? Or was it just the connection with Robin that kept us in each other's lives? "Are you okay?"

"Of course I'm not okay." There was a pause and then, "Can I come around a bit later?" Like the old days.

"Yes." I forgot the state I was in, how tired I was. "I'll make my way back now."

At home, I tried phoning Gemma's mobile in the interim. It was switched on. She had been charging it up. But it rang and rang and rang. Eventually, it defaulted to her voicemail. "Gemma, worried about you. Call me when you can?"

Then all I could do was wait for her to call back. Robin was buzzing my intercom. When I reached him, he was grey, leaning so far forward that I felt relieved that I had reached the door soon enough to prevent him from falling onto it. I said, "I've asked her to call me. I'm sure we'll hear from her soon." He stumbled in and landed on the sofa, boots and coat still on.

"It's over, isn't it?" he asked me.

I wanted to tell him that it wasn't, but it didn't seem fair. What did I know? I stood over him trying to work out what it was I could do to make everything better.

He looked up at my silence. Then I felt the awkwardness of the expression on my face, the shock and defeatedness that would answer him better than the words I had not used. I tried to change the look, but it was too late. He looked back down again. He didn't even sigh.

"Should I have gone after her that night?"

"I have no idea." I found I was frozen, standing there wearing that frown.

Why was Gemma doing this to him for just that one row? I knew she had strong ideas of how things should be, but this was extreme. And not to call me either.

"Wasn't the first time," he said as if answering my thoughts. "I turned up at one of her friends' parties. I'd had a bit of an absinthe episode and was kind of out of it."

"Yes, she told me. I'd forgotten. How had that happened?"

He turned to look up at me. "After you told me about a Mr Hawk in Ethiopia. I knew who it was, Bernie. I thought you did. I thought that was why you were telling me."

"You knew the facts?"

"No, but if havoc was being created in a country my dad had been in, chances were, it was my dad causing the havoc. That's without you giving me his name to pin it on."

I went to fetch the coffee, brought it to him and placed it on the coffee table. I sat on the floor next to the sofa.

"He was arrested last night. Did you know that?"

I nodded my head, ashamed of the way that the beer was still disorienting me. My head moved down and the image of the living room followed moments afterwards. "I just heard."

"You say you've left a message on her phone?"

I nodded. "Hopefully, she'll call back soon."

"I've left dozens of messages. She hasn't called me back yet."

He was stretched out on the sofa. I had thought he was the magician but he turned out to be the romantic hero. And now he wasn't even the hero, he was something else, something the fairy stories hadn't catered for. Perfect but depleted. I saw his eyes move towards my phone.

I didn't need Robin to say anything to justify being at my house. I don't think Robin needed me to speak to have the answers but the silence was awkward. "Shall I switch on the TV?" It'd make waiting for the call more bearable.

We sat watching over-bright scenes of the world, of London. Green football pitches passed our eyes as Battersea became greyer through the window behind the TV. "Have you been drinking?" he asked me suddenly.

I smiled, embarrassed. "I suppose so. A thing with work..." my voice trailed off.

"Oh." He turned back to the television. "I haven't," he said. It took me a moment to work out he meant he hadn't been drinking as if that could demonstrate that he wasn't the same person who had offended Gemma. I hoped that Gemma would call soon. It never occurred to me that she might not.

I'm telling the story of Gemma and Robin. I need the information to conclude the plot. So, we sat there, just waiting for Gemma to call me. Robin and I needed to be together for this. I needed to know the moment he heard from Gemma. I needed to know when Robin knew whatever there was for him to know. Or maybe, I just wanted Robin to be sitting there on my sofa.

The television ambled on, from light quiz shows to soaps. I hadn't seen this sort of thing for years. I was reminded of my front living room, years ago with my dad, chips and fish fingers on my lap. I can't imagine that happening in Canada. "You want something to eat?"

"What you got?"

"Chips, pasta, freezer food. Anything really."

He waited for a few moments. "Not hungry."

129

I thought that we were going to return to silence, but he said, "I did everything wrong."

"No, you didn't."

But he had started back on words again and he continued with words spiralling out like his mosaic. Now Robin was Sylvie from the film. I was Ben. I thought I should point out that this was not half as bad a role as had been implied from the film. I did not feel overburdened by him being there.

Robin's ideas were all over the place. It was like he had been waking in the night, mimicking my insomnia, as if he was scribbling graffiti on the walls with a 3B pencil, scribbled anger at himself and Gemma. This was how the pigeon ideas in his head were working. They were getting out of his head onto the new barrier of the walls. They were still grey, the colour of the pencil lead. They were still confined and though they were furious, he thought they were nothing much.

Talking to me was his other graffiti.

The call did not come. Robin did not leave. I left him, I suspect, not sleeping on my sofa. I slept without difficulty.

Chapter 17

How can I begin to tell you this part of the story? How do I begin? Because it fell into my life like a dead pigeon falling out of the air to my feet, with a phone call. The sort of thing that you take in logically and sensibly, knowing you should be upset but not knowing what to do about it.

So, do I start with the pictures of what happened? Or tell you how it unwound into my life. I think I can't do either. I'll try both.

At work, an old inbox flashed up, full mostly of junk, a couple of credit card statements. That'd make it two months that I hadn't checked this account. I scanned the rest of the contents. I saw Gemma's name, five from the top. Finally. I clicked on the name.

It was pinched and economical with words, like Gemma's small self. "Don't feel like talking. Gone to stay with relatives on the coast," it said. "Update you later." It was timed and dated to a few days ago. How neat that she should communicate with me like this, with nothing to offer Robin by means of hope or explanation. I couldn't ask by email why Gemma should close up so suddenly and snap off the fingers of something so beautiful. Small Gemma, shut up like a compact, leaving all the emotions to me. Didn't she remember I don't do emotion?

From the date of the mail, I could see that the update was already four days old. The next day, the sun began to come out. I was too annoyed to notice this could be an unreasonable length of time not to hear from Gemma now and when finally, the phone started ringing, I didn't recognise the number.

The voice at the end was a young man's. "I'm Gemma's brother. We met a while ago." I had visited Gemma's hometown a couple of times. I had a picture of a pale, skinny boy with dark eyelashes, could have been her brother, or just a childhood friend. I attached the image to the voice on the end of the phone.

"Gemma left her mobile here. We got your message yesterday. We didn't know what to do about it for a while."

Like a pigeon falling sudden and dead at your feet while you were living the rest of your life so normally.

"What do you mean?"

"There's been an accident."

132

How did it happen? She was on a pier, a long stone pier. I thought piers had shops and amusement arcades along them. Not all of them, Bernie. You're thinking of Brighton Pier. This was just a wide stone wall. Gemma wasn't shopping. She was taking in the elements. Her aunt and uncle were in a car nearby, at the pier's base, en-scarfed, en-gloved, filling their mugs with flask-cooled tea. They found it too cold and windy to get out of the car and join Gemma. The wind was focussed by the cliffs.

I mean, you'd think, wouldn't you, the tide's in, the sea is stormy – you know the sort of thing. The black of an angry sea is more ominous than any other natural element I have seen, and it was casting its punches against the stone of the pier, sea spray in the air. You'd think they'd see all that and say, "Gemma, it's not safe to walk along the pier right now." Maybe she'd find it exhilarating, but it wasn't safe, small rowing boats bubbling violently against the wall and cliffs.

But I suppose we forget the frailty of ourselves, our lives. And, possibly, as Gemma started walking out to the lonely white pole at the end of the pier, the weather had yet to take that particularly nasty twist when you know it's time to play it safe.

Sea spray on Gemma's pale skin, on each silky strand of her hair and the fibres of her jumper, exposed where she hadn't buttoned her denim jacket, sea spray on the windscreen of the car. Her relatives didn't look up. They heard the water spatter. It sounds like the fizzing of champagne. Maybe me and Mr Tadesse were drinking beer at that very moment. What was Gemma thinking? What had she said to her parents about Robin? I think she was thinking that she needed this time away to decide if she had a future with Robin or not. And I don't know what she had decided.

So, what? A particularly vicious push of wind? A large, unexpected wave? Something else? But when Gemma's relatives looked up from the drop of coffee forming a brown lump in the Tupperwared sugar, her uncle's, "Oops, sorry," and aunt's tut, still hanging in the air, Gemma wasn't on the pier anymore. She didn't seem to be anywhere.

And they got out of the car and called for her, even though in all that time of looking down and looking up, there was only one place that she could be. And I suppose they were crying. At the very least, her aunt was crying. Tears, red-veined cheeks and tightly permed fair curls. I suppose they thought about going after her, one of them probably tried to enter that world of frantic salt and hissing pebbles. And it was probably a good few minutes before it occurred to anyone to call someone – an ambulance, a doctor, the coastguard.

They found her, the coastguard that is, in the sea calm of the following afternoon, found her buffeted amongst seaweed by the waves in the cove. Her head was bruised, blossoming brown bruises over her eyes and forehead, perhaps from the fall, perhaps hitting the wall. But ultimately it was the water that had killed her – in her body, her stomach, her lungs. In all the places that oxygen should have been, there was saltwater.

Unlike love, death seems to be fair gain as far as narration is concerned. And she'd hurt me more this time. Gemma, why didn't you warn me that this was going to happen when we met, when we raced up the steps to the flat neither of us would ever rent, or when you bought Robin to my front door? Why didn't you wear the sign on your face: PR assistant, premature demise age twenty-four?

I had thought that Gemma would always be there. Not as an anchorage but as a buoy, a pointer to my location, however detached I was. I left the office, just leaving an awkward explanation with Craig. He frowned as he tried to sound understanding about something he didn't know about. The awkwardness chased me out of the door. I ran home.

"Where did you say she was?" I had called Robin. I had no idea if he would have known. I was perched on a stool, shaking in my cold, cold kitchen.

"Not far from Bournemouth."

"Her parents are there now?"

I nodded. "Or they will be. I think they have to identify the… "

"How am I going to get to Bournemouth?" His voice was desperate. "I have no idea how I can get there."

"You don't have to get there, Robin."

"Of course I do."

I could see his picture on my kitchen wall. Blurred and small but happy. "I'll drive you there, Robin. I'll just check with her parents first."

Robin knew grief before this happened. Grief, like seeing all the beautiful things in life in a mirror and then touching the reflected image of soft warm skin and recoiling at the cool of the glass. Maybe Robin's experience of grief before this had not been literal grief, but the aching hopelessness was captured in mosaic, the image that would inspire Sylvie to cope with the death of her husband.

So, what confused me was this. If Robin knew how terrible it could be, why did he elect to put himself through it? Did he think that he was immune to the world that he made in the cinema, that young deaths don't occur in the real mundane world?

I stared at him in the greasy spoon at the end of my road, his body utterly devoid of magic, ashen. I knew it wasn't right to ask him, but I burned with curiosity.

Perhaps it was Robin and his attitude to risk, running away to see the world and to make the mosaic. He'd said that's what he wanted and he'd take the consequences. I can't expect to understand. I own a house without ever having had a mortgage.

So maybe that's how he thought about Gemma. Robin wanted this and he wouldn't get it if he didn't take on the chance that he might ultimately lose.

I stared down at my plate. I had picked up a box of cornflakes and an apple. Even if I managed to push out the smells of cooked sausages and bacon and eggs from the kitchen, the cornflakes smelt terrible. I lifted the cup of tea to my face to steam out anything else. It was Lapsang Souchong. The smoky smell was a little better. Not great, but a little better.

"Why did we bother trying to eat?" asked Robin, indicating his equally untouched plate. He was leaning back from it also as if the smell repelled him.

"Do you want to sit in reception for a bit, instead?"

He nodded. We stood up. From a sense of not wanting to leave the table so completely untouched, I picked up my cup of tea. He just picked up his jacket.

The reception was grandly decorated for a three-star. The photo was on the front of all the promotional literature scattered on the tables. There were uplights and beautifully upholstered armchairs in front of the shiny oak reception. We sat in two chairs on either side of a coffee table with the FT and a glass ashtray. This was a bit more than I expected, but

I had had trouble finding rooms with so little notice. Many places were closed until the sun came out.

"When are you thinking of going back to London?" I asked.

In response to my question, he glanced up. I followed his eyes. A middle-aged couple carrying suitcases were standing at reception. "That's her parents," he told me. What is lost, what is left. Mental note to Bernie: either have lots of children or none at all, to better cope with loss. He sighed and stared at the ashtray. "Bernie, before we go and speak to them, I just want to remind you that I..." I was aching to hear what he needed to say. "I'm not sure that I was even Gemma's boyfriend anymore. They might not have heard of me. They might thing I'm the nasty ex-boyfriend. I don't know what they know or believe."

I nodded. "I never was Gemma's boyfriend."

He managed to smile.

"It'll be fine. Come on."

"Have you had all you came for?" I asked him. It was our second evening. We were eating fish and chips on the beach. But it wasn't night. It was a grainy, irritating dusk. There had been no sunset.

He nodded, but he said, "I don't know what I came for."

"But it's good that we came. Both of us." It felt right to do something. The thing I didn't know I had to do when I had run from work to find a purposeless house.

"This fish is rank," he said, politely removing a corner of it from his mouth.

"Well, I told you never to risk more than mushy peas."

"Do you think that they knew?"

"Who knew what?"

"Her parents. How things were with me and Gemma."

They'd had lunch with us. Kind of them, considering. We'd sat with a selection of handmade cakes on a silver stand in the centre of the table. There was a frog-shaped cake of green icing. I had as little appetite as everybody else right then but spent a long time stealing glances at its white fixed eyes, trying to work out why you'd want a cake shaped like a frog. The place had been crowded with kitchen noises and its elderly patron's voices raised to be heard by the hard of hearing. It was Gemma's brother I'd felt sorry for. Twenty-one, distinct from his parents by his age, and distinct from the London perspective of Robin and me, our stories, though not mentioning her, all coming from the same observation deck.

I think they knew. How could they not? But they hadn't acted or said anything differently. "If they did, they didn't care. You're never going to be a blip on the way to something else, now, are you?" Oh, why did I say that?

He was staring ahead. "No." We watched waves come in and go out. It was a few seconds before I reminded myself we were looking at Gemma's grave. "When do you want to go home?" he asked me, rescuing me from my brooding.

"It's your call."

"I'm tired now."

"What, now? Like now this minute?"

He rolled his head towards me. "Is that alright?"

"Of course. It's your trip."

He squeezed my knee. "I appreciate this. Would you give me a quarter of an hour? I mean, now?"

I nodded, wrapped up my chips without knowing where I'd finish them. "I'll meet you back at the hotel." I kissed his cheek. Wherever he went when I left him there, I'm not going to conjecture. I wandered slowly amongst the plastic toy souvenirs and stared at the windows of closed tea shops.

The presence of the sea reminded me of home. I reached instinctively for my phone at the recollection and hovered over my dad's number, before switching to text. "Thinking of you," I wrote, the first time I had ever reached out to them. "Hope you are settling in okay." Because maybe it was okay to paddle in the emotion.

I'd packed, was still sitting on the bed, staring at the peach walls wondering what to next when he finally knocked the door. He didn't look me in the eye as he came in. He was white, under-shaded with pink, like sore eyes.

"Already packed?" he asked, picking up his key from a chest of drawers and I nodded. "Best be going then."

Rucksack on my shoulder, suitcase in his hand, we handed the keys in at reception, signed for our bills and wandered to the car park.

"I'm dead tired," Robin said, once our things were in the boot. "Mind if I sit in the back?"

"Go ahead."

He was asleep, or acting it, across the back seats of the car. I say acting it because although he had been silent all the journey, when I turned in my seatbelt to look at him, I could see a streetlight glinting back from somewhere in his face.

It was as if Gemma was out there, suspended in H2O like a biological sample in a vast jelly. I pictured her as if I was looking up from the ocean floor and the brightness of the sun pushing through the opaque of the ripples was interrupted by her shadow. I couldn't imagine anything closer, anything more horrific. It was all very clean and peaceful. Sometimes I remembered that she would be white and cold and very horrible in a way that you cannot imagine if you have never seen a dead person and I tried to swamp out the thought with the vastness of the ocean vision I had conjured up.

Now Robin was left broken in my car. I was trying to find within myself the knowledge to know what to do. I didn't believe I had the power to make it all better, but just some expression, some action was required of me. I had buried my love a long, long time ago, marking it with a 'ready to wake up when it's needed' and then had to stamp even that proviso out as Gemma and Robin became closer. It wouldn't stamp out though. That 'ready to be woken up' wriggled and wriggled and squirmed out from underfoot until the whole grave of my love was irrevocably disturbed. I had to just take it out, allow all the grit and dirt to it and force it to look like something platonic. I guess the way I battered my love was unusual.

I didn't want to use this week as a reason to reverse all that, but it was freer and as I unfolded it, looking for direction on how to act, I found my love flummoxed.

I was struck by all the deep questions that come when you are lost in the dark. I knew where I was going tonight, under the signs telling me the miles to home. But I was lost in images of how anyone gets over this sort of thing. You hear on the news that these things happen, then they become vague memories.

Maybe it was selfish of me to wonder how to act. Perhaps I should have just noticed where I thought I could help and wait for him to accept it or push it away.

I wondered then if, in his confused state, he might turn to me. I resolved now to push him away. Like the sharp aggressive push of a boat from the shore into calm waters. And though the push would be violent, the boat would glide peacefully and happily. I could watch it from the bank. I could hope that he would see me smiling at him.

But I haven't told you about the last scene of the mosaic film, seconds before the credits, the one where the heroine 'achieves normality', as Robin put it. Well, I didn't think it was so worthwhile until now.

What did I hate about achieving normality? Conforming, relinquishing the spark like the one Robin has, even if a spark that might unhappiness.

And now, the night after our return to London, as I finish watching the film again, alone, half a bottle of Merlot on the floor, marvelling at his sequences and invention and then being confronted with that last scene, I realise I have to tell you about it.

On the screen, traffic flutters past and we see Sylvie, the heroine, climb onto a red bus. This bus even has a conductor to whom she flashes her pass and takes a seat. No, it's not a gratuitous cliché. This London isn't all punks and Princess Di. Sylvie swings to the side as the bus pulls away and bumps past the shops of what looks like a Saturday Brixton High Street.

She's changed her hair. Discrete highlights, I think, and it's tied back rather than limp around her face. So it's obvious that time has moved on and she's changed, not the clinging desperate woman we saw before. She's wearing make-up, reading a small article about the arrest of Ben and the murderers of Peter, overshadowed by an advert for BT above it. Sylvie's not smiling but she's calm as the last scene pans out, filling the screen with Robin's mosaic. Like a music of its own, the camera follows one of the bright bottle top roads to a ribbon to the mountains, a more optimistic place. Sylvie's tragedy has been resolved and suddenly I wonder if I had misunderstood what Robin had been saying.

Here is the beginning of normality. You don't realise how so many people in the world must be walking around under scars. You never question how things change. She looks normal, acts normal, she must believe she is living a normal life.

This what Robin actually meant by normality, not that Sylvie was conforming, but she was achieving a kind of peace despite tragedy. Sylvie's a young widow. Childless. Will she really never be strung out by emotion again? But we know, as Robin said we would, that she has achieved normality.

Robin is younger than Sylvia, by a decade, I'd guess. He has longer to reach this ideal state, move onwards whilst still holding onto his loss. I am glad for him.

But I have this time to move on too. I've learnt that trying to hide myself from losing Robin didn't stop me feeling the pain of losing him; that it didn't stop me losing Gemma. Despite the things dragged away from us, we can still look forwards, and find new stories. Maybe always there will be a bouncy-shoed Bernie haunting London through dusty records. Maybe there won't.

I glance at the phone. I want to call Robin to tell him that I finally understand. But not yet. A strange hope and fear hold me at the same time, as I begin to realise that if he comes close, I might not have to push him away.

I might even choose to reach out before then.

***

READ MORE ABOUT BERNIE in the FREE SHORT STORY, EVELYN: https://alexmorrall.com/adrift/

Review Request

If you've enjoyed reading **ADRIFT**, I would be very grateful for an honest review on: http://mybook.to/AdriftTheStoryteller

Reviews help booksellers identify which books to promote and help other readers find a book that they'd enjoy.

You can read a further extract from the life of Bernie and her friends for free, on:
https://alexmorrall.com/adrift/

Sign up to my Reading Club

Still thinking of Bernie and her decisions? Why not download some a short story from the original longer portion of ADRIFT describing how Robin's new relationship begins... https://alexmorrall.com/adrift/

Sue is a young professional just starting out in London. But when her boss Evelyn insists that Sue meet one of her potential clients on her behalf, worse, pretend to be Evelyn, she is railroaded into a meeting in which she might have found her soulmate, but one who will not know who she really is.
Told through the eyes of storyteller Bernie, the main character of ADRIFT, Sue and Evelyn's client will have an effect on Bernie's life that none of them ever expected.
DOWNLOAD for FREE at: https://alexmorrall.com/adrift/

The link will also give you the opportunity to sign up to my reader's club where you can stay up to date with new books, articles about the writing process, and give you a chance to join the conversation, plus freebies along the way. But if you don't want to stay in the club, just click unsubscribe when you get your free book.

A Note About the Story

I wanted to spend more time dwelling on Robin's trip to Ethiopia, reflecting my own surreal experience of my first time on an airplane for 13 years taking me to East Africa.

When the PA at the consultancy firm introduced me to one of the directors, with the words, "He wants to send you around the world," I was a little taken aback to discover they meant Ethiopia. Brought up in the eighties, I'm ashamed to say that Ethiopia only meant famine and desert to me.

The director hastily added we would be housed in a five star hotel, and indeed we were, one with six restaurants and several pools, which felt somehow wrong when on the streets we saw children carrying home newly dead dogs, but I was too shy and sheltered to enunciate this.

These days I will admit that I was too young to make the most of the experience. I had not been long in London, in my very first job, and was pretty overwhelmed to be sent away again. It takes a certain amount of entitlement to go out and explore a new country when you're told not to go without security, or to understand that you can really step in and embrace the culture. But my employer arranged horse-riding, which again highlighted that I was the only one inexperienced enough to not know how to horse-ride; a visit to Merkarto and its vivid pools of spices; a sight more common in this Instagramming age; and was taken to eat Ethiopian food.

In the evenings, to burn off the ridiculous quantities of all-inclusive (a concept I had never before encountered) luxury food, I would swim in the pool which was a darting experience of avoiding un-named bugs, legs frantically struggling to stay afloat. This was where I first discovered caviar, and Belgian chocolate mousse - no not together. Needless to say, my swimsuit grew smaller over the month

Feeling inadequate also made it hard to get involved with the work, and my daytimes were locked into the 'office' a square of desks where we all sat typing on humongous laptops, or in my case, trying to find prise jobs from the defensive managers. It was hard to email in those days, we would take it in turns to connect the unreliable modem, sometimes taking hours to download a single email, typically I received no personal email. There were people back home I thought about emailing, but surely they would have emailed me if they wanted to talk to me?

Occasionally I was sent on information gathering exercises amongst the company's staff, bemused by their concern about being judged due to a rogue fly that had entered the office, not noticing my fear of being judged as totally out of my depth. More fun was visiting the patisserie on the Churchill road, amongst Emerald skyscrapers. Patisseries were the new thing at the time, and everyone wanted a business in them. As apparently the only white people in Addis Ababa, eager strangers with a kind air would walk alongside us wanting to talk worldwide politics, the US, the Nile.

And what struck me most of all, other than the experience of the Ethiopian meal, the amber tej and pollo wot (hinting at

147

my future as a food reviewer), was that the crescent moon lies on its back on Ethiopia's side of the equator, a glowing cradle nestled in the mountains. Nobody had ever told me.

Sign up to my readers club and receive another story from Bernie's life for Free: https://alexmorrall.com/adrift/

Helen and the Grandbees

'Breathtaking and moving, *Helen and the Grandbees* is a novel that bravely explores themes of familial discord, race and love in modern Britain. It is a book that immediately gripped me, compelling me to keep turning the pages well into the night. Morrall writes with confidence, poise, and a sense of humour to match. At times heartbreaking and heartwarming, this is a novel readers won't soon forget. A riveting debut.' *Awais Khan, author of* In the Company of Strangers

'Alex can write; she has a way, a bit like playwright Mike Leigh, of zooming into the tiniest, seemingly mundane physical details of a situation, and in so doing, conveying the complexity, circularity and pattern of relationship and emotion. There is a humanity and a realism about her writing that Is far from commonplace despite the fact that when you read about the people and situations in her storytelling, they are instantly recognisable. *Helen and the Grandbees* is unbearably sad but because Alex manages the seemingly impossible feat of introducing hope right from the start it is possible to read and read on, with curiosity and enjoyment.' *Dr Kairen Cullen, Writer and Psychologist*

'Authentic and tender. This utterly moving novel has created an unforgettable heroine in Helen. I held my breath as her troubled life unfolded and wanted only the best for her and her grandbees. This gorgeous book is not just an exploration of identity, race and mental health, but also one about family love, sacrifice and bravery. I loved it.' *Carmel Harrington, International Bestselling Author*

'What an honor and privilege it has been to read *Helen and the Grandbees*. I enjoyed it immensely. Every single character was memorable and felt completely genuine. Alex Morrall is a hugely talented author, with a gift for drawing characters of vastly different ages and from various backgrounds and social classes... This is the type of novel that will stick with me for a long time.' *Mary Rowen, author of Leaving the Beach*

Read the first three chapters of Alex Morrall's debut novel HELEN AND THE GRANDBEES for free here: Read THE FIRST THREE CHAPTERS FOR **FREE** HERE:
   www.alexmorrall.com/free

or buy here: https://books2read.com/u/bWGMZz

About the Author

Alex Morrall was born in Birmingham and now lives in south-east London where her voluntary work inspired 'Helen and the Grandbees', which is based in the deprived areas of Deptford, and is about the strength of family love overcoming the most intimidating of barriers. She is also a published food reviewer and poet. She enjoys working using other her creative and mathematical background. She has a maths degree but paints beautiful city scenes and landscapes in her spare time.

Sign up to my mailing list below for updates and free extracts developing Bernie's story.

You can connect with me on:

- https://alexmorrall.com
- https://twitter.com/AlexPaintings
- https://www.facebook.com/alexmorrallwriterartist
- https://www.instagram.com/alexmorrall_author_art

Subscribe to my newsletter:

- https://www.subscribepage.com/z9r7l5

Also by Alex Morrall

Alex has a way, a bit like playwright Mike Leigh, of zooming into the tiniest, seemingly mundane physical details of a situation, and in so doing, conveying the complexity, circularity and pattern of relationship and emotion. There is a humanity and a realism about her writing that Is far from commonplace.' *Dr Kairen Cullen, Writer and Psychologist*

HELEN & THE GRANDBEES
https://books2read.com/u/mq15Nv
Forgetting your past is one thing, but living with your present is entirely different

"A Gorgeous book" - Carmel Harrington
"Uplifting & Engaging" UK National Press

Helen's baby 'her Bee' is knocking at her door twenty years after she had to give her up for adoption, and her bee has questions. Questions that Helen is unwilling to answer. In turn Helen watches helplessly as her headstrong daughter launches from relationship to relationship. When it's clear her grandbees are in danger, Helen must find the courage to step in, confronting the fears that haunt her the most. ***Step into Helen's tale here...***

REMEMBERING NOT TO BREATHE

https://books2read.com/u/m2lAvo

Five stories by Alex Morrall and Man Booker Shortlisted Clare Morrall

Bookish teenager, Ella is intimidated when she is asked out by an older boy on a motorbike. As she starts to get to know him, their tentative friendship is under threat by the shadows of misogyny around her school and on the streets. How can she work out where the boundaries of a healthy relationship lie?

Follow these characters and others, exploring themes of regret, and isolation in this collaboration between Alex Morrall ('A hugely talented writer' - Mary Rowen) and Man Booker Shortlisted, Clare Morrall.

Made in the USA
Las Vegas, NV
09 March 2022

45299919R00095